Reclaiming Buck

Alcoholism, a Young Man, and the Miracle of his Recovery

—A Novel

Reclaiming Buck

Alcoholism, a Young Man, and the Miracle of his Recovery

—A Novel

John A. Aschenbrenner

© 2007 John A. Aschenbrenner

Photography by the author

Interior and cover design by Belle Ink LLC

ISBN: 978-0-6151-4882-3

In cooperation with

Belle Ink LLC
Hartland, WI

John Aschenbrenner has also written:

REFLECTIONS IN ERIK'S GYM
© 2006 John A. Aschenbrenner
ISBN-10: 1411697596
ISBN-13: 978-1411697591

Acknowledgements

There are so very many people I have to be grateful for as I've come to complete *Reclaiming Buck*. In most respects, with a few exceptions, they are the people who have encouraged me in my writing of *Reflections in Erik's Gym*, my first novel on Alcoholism, Addiction and Recovery. My own personal recovery and writings have been deeply nourished by my wife, Jane and my children: Annie, Michael & Andrew. My friends in recovery, and especially those that I've met at recovery meetings, group therapy sessions, on retreats, and those with whom I work at a very effective Mid-Western treatment center – you've all provided me with such a wealth of inspiration.

I wish to thank my best friends Bruce Bentz and John Erickson for their fearless and dedicated editing, and Jack Magestro, my publisher His humor, friendship, and expert knowledge within the publishing field have provided the vehicle for me to get my message to you.

I wish to especially thank those men I've been blessed in being able to sponsor in their early and continuing recoveries. They help me keep the vision of my own need to keep recovery as uppermost in my life - fresh and alive. They remind me that alcoholism and addiction isn't a game of chance we play. It's a terrible disease that kills as brashly as any other. They remind me that a recovery blessed by each new day is not only viable, but is being so very courageously lived by so many everyday people. I respect them deeply. They do more for me than I could possibly do for them. They are among the most courageous men I've ever encountered…or ever will!

Thank you Jake, Bob,
John & Dominic

We
bring about
new beginnings
by deciding
to bring about endings.
To renew our lives
we must be willing to change,
to make an effort to leave behind
the things that compromise our wholeness.
The universe rushes in to support us
whenever we attempt to take a step forward,
to make ourselves more whole.
All the blessings that flow from God
stream toward us,
to bolster and encourage us,
because all Life is biased
on the side
of supporting
itself.

-Anonymous

I came
into Recovery
to save my ass,
and found my soul
connected to it.

- John Aschenbrenner

This book is dedicated to

Jake

who continues to honor me
in seeking out my sponsorship.
Jake keeps
the struggle and surrender into
Recovery alive in me.
He keeps it young,
reminding me
of my own roots-
those early days and months.
He continues to
afford me more
than I could
possibly offer him,
and his humility
will not allow him to see
how much he affords
those others
he touches
through his own
Recovery.

Reluctant Thunder

An early afternoon sun, filtering through the great windows looking out onto the fading perennial garden, fell behind threatening clouds that cast long shadows across the cluttered office. Though I believed the calendar hanging over the desk, my fear that our crisp vibrantly colored autumn was about to recede from Southern Wisconsin's landscape sent its' wary chill up my spine. The memory of our last and all-too-long winter with no spring was too fresh, and the possibility of its return caught me looking into the eyes of an annual depression that somehow always holds me captive during those long and dark months. "Seasonal Affective Disorder" is what they call it, but I was becoming suspicious of who *they* were, and tired of all the new diagnostic labels that seemed to feed the pharmaceutical companies' greed and marketing strategy for creating consumer need based on all-too-poorly defined diagnostics. It seemed just another excuse to feel poorly and to search out a quick fix. American materialism and its' manipulation of the consumer seems to have invaded the health care system, tying the hands of well-intentioned physicians, and making insurance companies that much more restrictive in their willingness to pay providers for services. It's not that I trusted insurance companies. I didn't, and often wondered if they weren't the greatest force driving and limiting Medicine. An exasperated doctor once told me, "John, the only thing you need to know about insurance companies and their regard for the patient, is that they'd rather see him dead! It's a lot less expensive. It's all about money." I never forgot his comment and have always remained suspicious about both insurance and pharmaceutical companies. The ringing phone jerked me out of my reverie and to attention.

"Huntington Recovery Center, John speaking."

"John," I recognized the voice immediately. It was Terry in Admissions. She had called earlier, telling me to expect a new admission to our treatment center. "We've got Robert here, and I've completed his initial admission. Can I bring him over?"

I checked the clock. The residents had just returned from art therapy and were now in the basement group room, involved in the morning group session with Gerry, the primary therapist. I had about an hour of quiet time before residents would be stopping in the office for medications or any of the other things they might need from me. "Sure Terry, bring him over."

"What room can I assign him?"

"Let's see," I checked the chart that contained the names of our residents, their rooms and those rooms that were vacant. "We'll put him near the office until we get to know him. Room 2 is vacant and was just cleaned this morning. Does he want to be called *Robert* or *Bob*?"

"Well" Terry paused, "Neither." There was another pause. "He likes to be called *Buck!*"

"Hmmm, great," I groaned. "How old is he?"

There was a muffled chuckle on the other end, and I knew the new admission was in earshot of Terry. "He's twenty eight, and this is his first time in treatment. He's a trainer at one of the gyms in the area."

"And what's his *drug of choice*?"

"Alcohol, though he suggests he uses pot recreationally."

"Right; and the Bavarian Pope prefers to use beer rather than wine when he celebrates Mass!"

Terry cleared her throat, choking back the laugh and maintaining her professional stance. "I'll have him to you in a couple of minutes." She hung up and I reached for a new chart, ready for the patient to be entered into its pages, and into the cupboard for the Polaroid camera. We'd need a photo for the med book. It was our way of identification.

I thought about my cynical remark to Terry. She knew I believed in our mission of helping people deal with their dependency issues, and of my own earlier struggles with alcoholism. She also knew how frustrated I felt about the lady who had discharged AMA, against medical advice the day before, and just when we thought she was making a breakthrough in coming to understand her complete uncontrollability when it came to alcohol, or any other mood-altering substance. Once through, she would be *workable*, and we could begin helping her on her journey into ongoing recovery. But she *wasn't* ready, and fell back into her remarkably well- constructed system of denial. "We've at least planted the seed," Gerry said, "and drinking will never be the same for her. With a little Divine Providence, she'll hopefully and eventually get it." My problem was not being able to sometimes maintain a professional distance, allowing my efforts to become enmeshed in the plight of the patient, and feeling frustrated when those efforts were thwarted. There was something about a young guy named Robert entering treatment and wanting to be called "Buck." It smacked of his drawing the proverbial "line in the sand." I hoped I was wrong. Thunder rumbled over the treatment center as I pulled the necessary blank documents from the chart, found the necessary lab tests requests from the file, and grabbed the plastic-packaged urine specimen cup from the lower cupboard. A final flash of lightning followed by an immediate clap of thunder opened the skies and a downpour began its' mighty crescendo against the windows. I heard the front door open and went to the office door, looking down the corridor as Terry and a tall man with a suitcase and duffle bag pushed into the refuge of Huntington House.

"Whew, just got in," declared Terry! The pair drew closer, Terry leading the way. The new admission was a strong-featured and well built young man, which usually wasn't the case with an alcoholic entering treatment for the first time. Usually they were undernourished and emaciated. Perhaps his young years were still working on his side, and given that he was a trainer, he may have continued to try to keep himself nourished. He carried both himself and his belongings with a certain thrusting arrogance, though one could easily see the slight twitch in his cheek and the nervousness in his eyes, darting his gaze down the hall and into the office, checking me out like a tired warrior would his captor before being taken prisoner. I felt a measure of compassion, and held out my hand before Terry made the introduction.

"Hi, my name's John. Welcome to Huntington."

Terry jumped in, "John, this is Robert."

The young man grimaced at Terry and then my way, "It's *Buck!* I like to be called Buck." He grabbed my hand, affording me an overly firm but nervous grip, pulling back immediately. He grimaced again, recognizing his obvious shakiness.

"OK, *Buck* it is." Turning to Terry, "Has Buck had his physical exam and do we have doctor's orders?"

She handed me a sheaf of papers. "John, everything you need is in here. Do you have an umbrella I can use to get back to the main hospital?"

I pointed to the stand near the door. "Are you in a hurry? Why not wait this out? The weather report is for a driving rain, bringing in a cold front."

"Probably the end of our autumn color; it'll take the remaining leaves from the trees. Can't stay though, I've got another admission to the Detox Unit waiting. It's been a busy day." Looking toward Buck as she headed to the door, "Good luck, Buck, you're in a good place. Some will say this is the finest treatment center in the Midwest!"

"We'll see," Buck groaned. He followed me into the office as I motioned him into a chair beside the desk. He fell into it, its back thudding against the wall."

I couldn't resist, "Almost knocked that chip off your shoulder, Buck."

He reddened, as a shaking right leg drummed the carpeted floor. I wished I hadn't made the comment and questioned my own need to mark my territory before the new dog in the neighborhood did. He glared at me and then looked away with a half-resigned sigh. His blue eyes began to tear, but he just as quickly regained his guard. "Look! Just teach me to drink and I'll be OK. Just need to be more careful. If it wasn't for that god-damned cop pulling me over and my wife, I wouldn't be here. Just need a fucking tune-up and a couple lessons in drinking." His eyes again caught mine and then darted away as they again began to tear. "Just, just fucking teach me!" Buck tried to choke back the emotion that was overtaking him, his leg affording an even fiercer cadence.

Suddenly I felt a shallow sense of hope. His emotions were opening, no matter how hard he tried to fight them. I softened in my tone, feeling a sense of compassion. "Buck, Buddy, it'll be OK." I paused for a moment, thinking about what I was about to say, and then shrugging my shoulders, "I've been through it too."

"What?

"Buck, I'm a recovering alcoholic. Actually I came through this program here in Huntington House, a little better than seven years ago. This place saved my life, and now I feel so very fortunate to be able to be part of the therapy team."

Suddenly I had Buck's full attention. "So now you're able to drink responsibly, and stop after a couple, like everybody else out there does?"

"I no longer drink alcohol, Buck. For me I've come to believe that one drink is too many, and a thousand could never be enough."

Buck's face jerked back as he tensed. "That's bullshit, fucking bullshit. I just don't know how to drink like everyone else. If you're not going to teach me, I'll have to just..."

The phone rang, cutting Buck short in mid sentence. He broke his angry stare, arching forward, nervously cupping his head and bracing his elbows on his knees. I though he was going to bolt and was surprised when he didn't. I grabbed the phone, "Hello, Huntington House. This is John."

"John, this is Gerry. I'm downstairs in group. I just got a page from the Detox Unit. They're wondering if I can come over to evaluate a newly arrived lady for Huntington. They say she won't stay if we're not going to take her following her detoxing. I wouldn't ask you this, but wonder if you could finish leading the group this morning. You'd just have to keep everyone engaged. I was about to introduce Peter the mortician, our new admission yesterday. I already know his story from interviewing him, and he just needs to outline his reason for being here to the group. What do you think? I'd owe you."

"Hmmm, don't you owe me from before, and before that?"

"OK, OK, you're right!" Gerry laughed and paused. "So you'll do it?"

"Sure, if I can bring Buck, our new admission, down to the group room with me? I can finish his paperwork later."

"Buck? Who's Buck? We were expecting a Robert somebody."

"He goes by Buck." Buck's nervous eye caught mine, wondering what the continuing problem with his name was."

"Oh, great; sounds like a pretty tall pedestal he's hanging himself from."

"You could say that, Gerry. We'll be right down." I hung up the phone and as luck would have it Buck didn't pursue his questions about being taught to drink. "Buck, we'll finish this later. I've got to cover our therapist's group while he goes over to the Detox Unit. It'll give me a chance to introduce you to the house."

A flash of lightening illuminated the office like a strobe at a dance. The clap of thunder following ushered in another downpour plummeting against the large office windows. I grabbed my keys and led the way, locking the office door behind us. Not saying a word, Buck followed me down the stairs and into the group room. The eyes of the group shifted from Gerry to me as we approached, entering their closed circle. I quickly introduced Buck to Gerry.

"Welcome to Huntington," Gerry looked directly into Buck's nervous gaze and then pointed toward the group, "Everyone's waiting to meet you," and then passing me, "John I owe you double for this!"

"Hmmm, when have I heard that before?" The group laughed, all except for Peter, who was about to introduce himself and his reason for being in treatment.

The group room afforded a large area able to hold a circle of chairs to accommodate two dozen residents when the house is full. It was comfortable enough, carpeted, with pleasant paintings covering the walls, a framed poster of *The Twelve Steps of Recovery*, and a framed listing of feelings, *Mad, Glad, Sad, Angry, Ashamed and Hurt,* which helped the newcomer identify feelings that have been denied or blunted through the use of alcohol or drugs. The group numbered thirteen, and Buck was about to find himself added to its number. He became visibly shaken, his eyes downcast as he entered the circle, taking a chair beside me.

"Hi, everyone; guess you have to put up with me for awhile."

"John, you can take our group anytime," Maxine, in her early 60's suggested, through a smoker's cough. I truly liked Maxine; a brazen self-willed woman who only thought after she spoke, and who was into taking everyone's but her own inventory.

I smiled, "Sucking up again, eh Max...?"

"Honey, you'll know it when I'm sucking up," she choked another raspy laugh, and the group laughed with her.

"Everyone, I'd like to welcome Buck, who's joining us at Huntington today. I know you'll help make him feel at home and help him through the schedule this first day."

Almost in unison the group rang out, "Welcome Buck!" and gave him a round of applause. Embarrassed, Buck reddened, nervously nodding his thank you.

I turned toward Peter, a man of 42, dressed in a pair of worn khakis and sweatshirt. "Gerry tells me you're about to tell us what brings you here." The group grew intently silent as Peter grabbed the sides of his chair so forcefully his knuckles turned white.

"I'm Peter, and I'm *thinking* I might have a problem with alcohol." It wasn't an unusual response for someone just entering treatment, and within a few days he probably would be introducing himself *as* an alcoholic.

"Hi Peter," came the group's response.

"I…ah, I seem to have gotten myself in a bit of a jam over the past week. I work," Peter paused, "Well I guess I'd better put that in the past tense. I *worked* for The Flowing Springs Funeral Homes in the Fox River Valley, just North of Milwaukee. I received a phone call this morning telling me I've been terminated. The corporation has three mortuaries in two different counties. I'm a licensed mortician and embalmer, and worked and lived in their Oshkosh home, though helped out in others when things got busy."

The group grew intent on his story, many leaning forward, myself included. I had heard there was a large incidence of alcoholism among people working in mortuaries, but this was the first mortician I had encountered at Huntington. This wasn't going to be your usual "hitting the bars too often" after work introduction.

"No shit, a real live undertaker," Jim from across the circle blurted out."

"Jim! We don't talk like that here. We need a little courtesy for Peter. It's difficult enough acclimating to treatment without…"

"Sorry Peter, I didn't mean anything by it," Jim cut me off, but seemed truly apologetic. He was a younger man, and still caught up in the impulsivity of his addictive behaviors.

"It's OK. Being a mortician has its ways of distancing a guy from *Joe Average* out on the streets, even when I'm in my jeans and out of my dark suits. But as I was saying, this past week things took a turn for the worse in my life. I'm always so careful about not drinking when I'm out in the public, but last Wednesday night things caught up with me. It was a long day of helping three families decide on funeral plans for their recently departed, picking out caskets, and the usual disbelieving 'It costs how much?' causing me to shift down into a cheaper gear, showing them something in nicely varnished pine as opposed to the upper-end Cadillac send off boxes with the embroidered silk interiors. I had had it, thinking it was only mid-week, and that I still needed to embalm a female corpse in the basement, and get her to one of our other homes in the next county for the hairdresser by seven AM so her visitation could begin in the early afternoon."

Peter looked out over the group, many transfixed by words painting images they never imaged they'd hear in a treatment center. Included in the group were two physicians and an attorney who understood death and dealt with grieving families in their day to day practices. The other members cast varied looks of dismay on listening to Peter's experiences bordering on things that just weren't talked about.

"Hey it's like anything else, and perhaps a business more necessary than most. So many people would like to deny our funeral homes are even in the neighborhood, walking past as if we were some phantom establishment that only appeared when necessity called, and then just as quickly again denied when the service is over and the hearse is again parked behind closed garage doors. Anyway, after the last family left, I turned on the phones answering machine, took off my tie and suit jacket, pulled on my white scrubs top and headed downstairs. It gets lonely down in the embalming room, and before I busied myself in preparing Bertha, I…"

"Bertha?" Maxine cackled, "You've got to be kidding!"

"Maxine," I gently turned toward her, "let Peter continue."

"No, no, it's OK. Undertakers always have their pet names for the corpses. For me, if it's a female it's a Bertha. A male is always Bruno."

"I'm sorry again, but you *have got to be putting me on!*"

Again I looked disapprovingly at Maxine, who just as quickly dismissed me.

"No, honestly, it's like anything else. We don't become emotionally attached to the corpses we work on. If we did, we couldn't deal with it, day in and day out. It's difficult enough having to put on our sympathetic faces when the family and friends arrive for services. I think most of us reserve the names for those who are elderly. What's really rough is when we have young people, and the most difficult bodies to work with are the infants. It's so hard remaining emotionally detached, as I'm certain it would be for a doctor who loses a young patient." Peter looked over at the two doctors who looked at each other, whispering and nodding knowingly. "Not only is my work lonely, it's boring. Imagine yourself working in a dead quiet room, doing things you could do with your eyes closed."

"And sometimes, from funerals I've been to, it looks like you guys do!" Maxine blurted out again. Everyone laughed including Peter.

"Max..." I begged, but myself having to smile.

"OK John, I'll keep my mouth shut," she rasped, clearing her throat.

Buck seemed to be relaxing beside me, perhaps as caught up in the unfolding story as the rest of us were, forgetting for the moment that he was just becoming part of this professional group of alcoholics and addicts attempting to save their lives. Initially I had thought it somewhat pretentious that a treatment center would cater to the professional population. Though I was an educated and professional man, when myself an inpatient I was at times intimidated by the doctors and other upper-crust professionals I encountered in treatment. Of late I began to believe there was a certain need for such a treatment center, as in many ways our lot was a more difficult one to treat. I leaned into Buck and whispered, "You doing OK?" He grunted and nodded.

"Really, if it's excitement in a career you're looking for; Mortuary Science isn't a vocation to pursue. Anyway, I try to emotionally detach myself from my work, and keep a fresh bottle of vodka behind the embalming fluids."

"Ever grab the wrong one?" Catching herself before I could say a word, she slyly smiled her huge grin my way, "Last time, John, I promise!"

"I'd figure it out soon enough! I pour myself a few ounces and the work becomes a bit easier and time seems to flow more quickly. By the time I was finished with Bertha, I had her completely dressed, her upper areas covered in plastic sheeting so the hairdresser didn't need to be so very careful, and had her hoisted into a transporting casket that we use when moving a corpse between our locations. My work for the evening was done, and I knew I was free until six AM when I needed to bring Bertha up in the elevator and move her into the back of the old hearse we keep for these simple purposes. A piece of cake, or so I thought. My wife was visiting her sister with the kids, and I had the place to myself. I washed up and took my half empty bottle of vodka up to our living quarters on the second floor. It was about 6:30 when I put away my suit, and got into my baggy UW football sweats, heading into the living room with a fresh glass of ice, my vodka and a new bottle of Roses Lime Juice. There's nothing like a tart vodka gimlet to take the edge off the day and relax into the evening. I put on some 60's and 70's CDs and picked up the paper. The words were a bit of a blur, so I settled for this month's issue of Men's Health. If the words were blurred, at least I could make sense of what was written with the photos. The first gimlet led to the second, and I shut my eyes, going back in time to the sounds of Motown and The Temptations. It was after the third gimlet, my vodka bottle empty, and in the middle of The Eagles singing "Desperado," imagining myself on horseback coming home from riding the fences in the depths of winter, that the shit started hitting the fan."

Peter paused, almost wishing he could go back into last Wednesday night and change what he was about to report. The silence continued, and Peter became more anxious and teary eyed, as the rest of the group edged ever closer, still in disbelief of the story that was unfolding.

Maxine couldn't contain herself, "Well, *what* happened?" I let her remark pass, myself as intent as the others.

"The phone rang. I thought not to answer it, as it was our private line into our living quarters. Thinking it might be my wife, I thought even more intently about not answering. But curiosity got the better of me, and I took the call. The voice on the other end was terse. I recognized it as the owner of the mortuaries, 'Where the hell are you? Where's the corpse? It's near
8 PM. I already owe the hairdresser for an hour, and she wants to go home. You were due here at 7PM!'"

I gulped and groaned, "You're kidding! My schedule has me bringing her over by seven in the morning."

"Have you been drinking? You sound slurred. You sure you can drive?"

"I'm fine,' I told my boss. 'You caught me taking a nap. I'll be there as fast as I can.' I hung up the phone, pulled on a pair of worn tennis shoes and my baseball cap, and bolted down the stairs, stumbling and nearly catapulting head first into the stairwell, catching myself on the rail, and pulling a tendon in my shoulder – thought I damned near pulled my arm out of its' socket."

"Peter,' I cut in, 'we've got about fifteen minutes, and then we have to go over to the dining room."

"I'll hurry this along. Within 20 minutes I had Bertha in the old hearse, hit the garage door opener and was flying down Main Street, heading for the Interstate and the next county. The tail lights on the car in front of me blurred into two pair, and I strained my eyes and neck to keep my head straight and my eyes in focus. I thought I was doing OK and merely had to bring the hearse back over the center line a couple of times."

"My god, Peter, you could have been…"

"Maxine, the only thing I was thinking about was a pissed off boss and getting Bertha prettied up with a nice "blow and go," for her sendoff. I thought things couldn't get any worse, until, well until they did! My rearview mirror became a blaze of lights! Red, white and blue; I thought it was the 4th of July, and then the sirens – Oh, those painfully loud sirens. I realized I was way over the center line in the left lane, veered the 1950's Cadillac Special over into my lane and hit the brakes too quickly. The squad car veered across the center line to avoid hitting me. I came to a stop and considered locking my doors and not talking to the cop until I sobered up."

Again, Maxine, biting her lip, leaned in, almost falling off the edge of her chair. "You have got to be kidding!" Thinking Maxine a lost cause for the moment, my own heart was racing. The room became as quiet and solemn as a tomb. Peter paused to collect himself, and all that could be heard were the intent and quickened breaths of everyone in the group. Moments turned into minutes as we sat on Peter's next words. Finally they came.

Looking out and into everyone like a preacher about to instill the wrath of God, he continued. "Now I've *really* got a problem." Another long pause, with everyone slowly nodding, until Maxine again couldn't contain herself.

"No shit, Peter!" That brought a few snickers, but the group continued to hold on in anticipation.

"I rolled down my driver side window and the rest is history. I think the cop thought I was one of those freaky kids who buy an old hearse for effect, and was a bit amazed to see an older guy in a shabby sweat suit and sneakers. I failed the field sobriety test with flying colors, and after he told me that my vehicle was being towed, I felt it my duty to explain to him, as best I could, the enormity of the situation.

As he peered into the back of the hearse, and turned green, I heard him exclaim under his breath, 'Oh fuck! Wait till the guys at the station hear about this!'"

"No shit!" Maxine exclaimed again.

"Max...!" I admonished, "Be a lady!"

"After a story like that? Who are you kidding?" She coughed and cackled.

Peter again looked out over an astonished group. "My boss was called, another hearse was sent out and the body was transferred, and the old hearse was towed into police custody. And that's it. When my wife found out, I knew if there was a chance to save the marriage I'd have to get my ass into treatment."

I began to thank Peter for being so open with us, and quickly realized he hadn't given up the platform.

"And if it's true that there's a greater incidence of alcoholism among morticians, one of our secrets is that it's easier for us to clean up after ourselves."

Buck, next to me, blurted out in dismay, "What's that supposed to mean?"

"We *never* have a problem getting rid of the bottles."

Dead silence filled the room. Even Maxine dodged the opportunity for a smart remark, her eyes wide in dismay, "And you introduce yourself with 'And I'm thinking *I might* have a problem with alcohol?' Honey, take off your shoes and get comfortable! Welcome to Huntington!"

II

A New Playing Field

There was little that appeared clinical about Huntington House. Sure we had cupboards with medications and individual bins of things residents couldn't keep in their rooms, such as car keys, over the counter medications and preparations that included alcohol. We had racks of patient charts and an office where Dr. Segen saw the patients at least weekly, but that was about all that reminded anyone we were under the governance of a psychiatric hospital. Many of the residents have described Huntington as a-sort-of-large-fraternity-sorority house. It *was* an old Victorian building, having originally housed staff working at the hospital during the beginning of the prior century when the psychiatric hospitals were considered sanitariums, and their *cures* were advertised to be more *the needed rest* away from the demands of society, in the country air and serene and confidential setting of lake and woods. It was a time when psychiatry was in its' infancy, and afforded only to the wealthy. The house had its' certain character; wonderfully windowed rooms, ancient woodwork, and decorated to afford a welcoming and homey setting. Group rooms doubled as TV lounge and sitting areas for visitors, and a kitchen and dining area with pantries stocked with snacks made both the resident and visitor feel welcome.

The weekdays afforded a complicated schedule of therapies and expectations, and a new resident kept checking that schedule for the first week, trying to not be late for group, art, or recreation therapies, along with juggling their own personal schedules of individual meetings with Gerry, Dr. Segen, Deb the family therapist, or those more mundane things that need to be completed over the course of any week, like doing laundry and heading to town for things they needed. The day started early with residents choosing to either walk over to the hospital for breakfast in the dining room, or having cereal and juice in the house kitchen. Some skipped breakfast, grabbing a quick coffee, but the expectation was that everyone began their day together at 7:30 downstairs in the large group room with morning meditation. It was a time for setting their individual focus and defining daily personal, therapeutic and family goals - challenges they were to consider throughout the day. The treatment day ended with 9:30 evening reflections, when residents considered a chosen and read meditation, and how they were able or unable to meet the goals defined in the morning. Weekdays were exhausting, and most of the free time was filled with individual assignments relating to the 12 Steps of Recovery, working on soul-searching autobiographies to be presented in group, and beginning to work on mending relationships with family and friends who visited during the short visiting time in the late afternoon and early evening following dinner. Included in all of that, the treatment expectation included all residents needing to attend a 12 Step Meeting, whether that's AA – Alcoholics Anonymous, or NA – Narcotics Anonymous. Occasionally there were specific individual treatment recommendations for given individuals to attend GA – Gamblers Anonymous, or SA – Sex Addicts Anonymous.

In contrast, the weekend was entirely different. Huntington seemed to relax; even the house creaked differently, relieved that the hurried pace had slowed for everyone to catch their breaths. But this Saturday, except for the ferocious weather, seemed almost too quiet and the treatment center almost too laid back.

The closing weeks of autumn did more than hint at a winter that threatened to storm in like some angry lover; her winds trying to shake Huntington House on its' foundations. Trees that surrounded the house were nearly bare of the leaves that slowed the winds, and creaked a foreboding welcome as did the stairs I climbed to reach the front door.

I had promised Dale on the PM shift that I'd cover for him; he needing to be out of town for a family funeral. It was a good weekend to be inside, and the treatment center had an intimate feel to it, like some great refuge from the addiction storms that so many people in our society were finding themselves caught up in. Normally I didn't work weekends, but we were always careful to cover for a fellow staff member when we could, as we never knew when we might need them to return the favor, and I didn't mind the pace of the PM shift as we were always double staffed, given the need to drive residents to recovery meetings while the other staff remained back with newcomers restricted to the house until they were more comfortable in their treatment and surroundings - and were trusted. I was working with Rebecca, and always enjoyed her quick wit coupled with a deep sense of compassion. Hers was a good mix in dealing with residents, and she seemed to have an uncanny nose for dishonesty, something all newcomers to recovery needed to free themselves of. She had a remarkable way of *taking the edge off* residential treatment, especially those new to the halls of Huntington. She spent a great deal of time interacting with them, especially the females, and I tried to afford the guys my time. There were also times we spent in small groups where the sexes were mixed, and both of us seemed comfortable enough in those settings. But this Saturday Huntington was *too* quiet and I had decided to do something about it, but before I could the front door opened and Angel entered, carrying bags and letting the cold wind slam the door shut with a bang behind her.

Angel was a twenty-three year old, already divorced, who had been a resident for the past two weeks. She'd been having a difficult time adjusting to the rules, and had a good many *boundary* issues, having taken a liking to both Jim and Buck. Though Jim was single, Buck wasn't, though that didn't stop her suggestive moves and advances. She stopped at the office to have us look through her packages and jacket, which she had taken off. Both Rebecca and I eyed the immediate problem before us, even before going through her bags. I allowed Rebecca the honors.

"Angel, you can't be wearing spaghetti straps and tops that allow an exposed midriff, and don't you think it's a little late in the season for *hot pink!* You know the rules; they're spelled out in the handbook! Did you leave with that on?"

Angel handed over her car keys, "Oh Rebecca, you know it's cute, and it's not like I'm *hanging out* all over! I bought it at that little boutique in the village mall."

"Might be cute on the beach, but not in a treatment center; a lot of vulnerable people here that might get the wrong…"

Angel winked, "I know, and a couple are really hot!"

Rebecca frowned, "Angel, you can't…"

"Oh, Rebecca, I'm just kidding. I'll put my sweatshirt back on."

"Hmmm, does it have spaghetti straps?" Not waiting for a response, Rebecca pointed to Angel's bags, "Let's go through these quickly. Where have you been, to *all* the stores in the village?"

"No, just got some things I needed for the week." Rebecca quickly looked through Angel's purchases, which included the usual things you'd find brought into a treatment center: cigarettes, toiletries, and those things that were more specific to Angel: two bottles of perfume, lace bikini briefs, lift-and-separate bras, two low cut cashmere sweaters, and a pair of jeans you'd need a crowbar to get into. Rebecca pulled out two articles: a non-aerosol bottle of hairspray, and a bottle of cologne.

"We'll need to keep these in your bin here in the office, and you can ask for them and then return them to us when you're done using them."

"But why the…"

"Because their main ingredient is alcohol and because they're non-aerosol it's too easy to get to the contents. We just need to help you and the others to be safe while in the house."

"What, you think I'd be drinking perfume and hairspray? You can't be serious?"

I took the lead, "Angel, we've had worse, and although it hasn't happened here, at a treatment center in Rhinelander a guy mixed gas he siphoned from his car with milk, drank it and died. It's just one of the house rules for everyone's safety."

"Gas and milk, now there's a new one; bet it goes over big during Happy Hour at your local tavern!"

I ignored the comment, sending Angel on her way, "And don't forget the sweatshirt!" Listening to her drag her bags down the hall, we heard her open the doors to the TV lounge, "Hi Guys!" followed by Jim's approving whistle.

"*Angel, the sweatshirt, please; now!*" Rebecca shouted down the hall!

Jim responded from inside the room, "Spoilsport! It's Saturday, we could use a little entertainment!" The doors closed and Angel continued on her way to her room.

"OK, OK, a sweatshirt it is! Maybe I'll pull my hair back and into a bun and find a dress down to my ankles!"

Looking at Rebecca, "And what was I saying about it being too quiet around here? It gets exciting pretty quickly, I'd say!"

"Careful John, You're married. *Remember?*"

"OK, OK!" I changed the subject, "Rebecca, do we still have Trivial Pursuit in the group room bookcase?"

"Hmmm, I think I'm going to spend my time with some of the residents; maybe Angel could use some time."

"No, not for *us* to play; I'm thinking of getting a game going at the kitchen table with the residents. Seems like things are too quiet with half the people on weekend pass"

"Think you'll get people wanting to play? You know how treatment people are, and trying to get them to begin having fun without drinking or using is like teaching a reluctant kid to ride a bike!"

"I know, maybe I'll have to do some dragging. We'll see." I headed out the office and down the corridor to the TV group room, pushing open the French doors.

"Hmmm, this is a sorry sight," I laughed. Peter in his UW sweats and baseball cap, and Charles, the African-American Attorney were sitting on the edges of their chairs watching the last quarter of the football game, while Buck laid full length and sprawled on the couch, seeming exhausted after his first week of treatment. Maxine looked up from her reverie, sitting back in the recliner, reading a romance novel and fantasizing about *what might have been* in her life, while Jean and Dave, our two doctors were working on their autobiographies and discussing how much they drank and used during their days in medical school. Jim, sunk deep and relaxing back in a bean bag chair had returned early from weekend pass, saying he was craving too much to be spending the weekend alone, even though he was to visit his parents in the evening. He had found a good level of security here at Huntington.

Maxine, as was expected was the first to respond, "Honey, what did you *think* this is; the waiting room for the stars ready to hit the stage and receive their academy awards?" She hacked her usual cough, rasping a laugh. Jean and Dave left their conversations, laughing at Maxine's quick humor.

"Go, go, GO! Yes!" Peter jumped to his feet, slapping Charles on the back. "Look at those Badgers go! It's another touchdown for Wisconsin!"

Buck threw his legs over the side of the couch, sitting, "What's the score?"

"28-14 – Wisconsin; it's too late for Michigan to pull this one out," Peter relaxed back into his chair.

"Trivial Pursuit on the kitchen table at 7 PM. I'll order in pizza for us! Do I have any takers?"

"What, *Trivial Pursuit?* You mean that board game? You've got to be kidding, John?" Buck moaned in half-awakened consciousness.

"Pizza, can I bring the beer?" cackled Maxine. Another laugh filled the room.

"Don't think so, Maxine; you sure you're *getting with the program*? Maybe we need to put you on the list to pick out the Christmas tree for the house," I teased.

"Honey, if I'm still here at Christmas, I promise I'll *be* the god-damned tree."

"Guys, it might be fun. I haven't played that game in fifteen years. I used to be almost addicted to it," suggested Dave, the doctor.

"You guys decide, but let me know early who's joining us so I'll know how much pizza to order." I pulled the doors closed behind me as I backed out of the room. Somehow I knew most everyone would be there, not wanting to pass up the pizza in comparison to the hospital food, regardless of how much they might not want to play the game.

By 7:15 while Rebecca covered the office and completed the charting I hadn't done, we were assembled around the great oak kitchen table, grabbing for slices of pizza and choosing up sides, two to a team. Maxine and Jean, Charles and Peter, Buck and Jim, and Dave joined me as we rolled the dice determining the first team to play and then following clockwise.

Charles landed on green - Science & Nature, and any of the opposing teams could read the question; whoever grabbed the box of cards first. Maxine reached the first card, "OK, Boys," Maxine strained her eyes, her glasses perched low on her nose, "What part of the human body is most commonly bitten by insects?" Maxine looked over her glasses, "Suppose they consider what might be hanging out at unwarranted times?" She got the usual snickers.

"Maxine," I chided. Let's keep it clean! I'm assuming they mean *clothed* people."

Charles looked at Peter, "Well, Mr. Undertaker, any ideas?"

"What, the attorney doesn't have a clue?" Peter ribbed his partner. "I'm guessing, given the mosquitoes here in Wisconsin, it's the forehead, if we're assuming the of the rest of the body is clothed."

"Is that your answer?" Maxine rolled her eyes as they agreed.

"Nope, it's the foot! See John, they're considering people who aren't wearing shoes!"

"Hmmm, guess you're right, but your mind all too quickly takes to the sewer."

"Hey!"

Jean and Maxine went next, landing on the brown - Art & Literature. Jean was an OB-GYN doc, and liked the science questions. "Mary, I hope you know something about this category. I'm a little shaky with the Arts."

"Honey, girls got to know about a lot of categories to survive!" She hacked another laugh.

Peter reached for the question, "Who wrote 'Women in Love'?"

Maxine slammed the table with her palm, "Men in need!"

The entire table, except for Buck, fell off into raucous laughter, and I couldn't help myself, joining in. "Damn it, Maxine, you've got the bawdiest sense of humor." I eyed Buck curiously, and he avoided my eyes. I was beginning to feel uneasy for him.

"I know, I know, like some old Irish barmaid I've been told."

"Hmmm, might not be far from the truth!"

Peter brought the group back to the task at hand, "Is that your answer?"

"Well of course not, Honey! Kick back a bit, and lighten up! There's nobody for you to embalm tonight; loosen your undertaker's tie!"

Peter grabbed the worn collar of his sweatshirt, pulling it away from his neck, as he would a tie. "Let me repeat the question. Who wrote 'Women in Love?'"

Jean beamed with excitement, "Although I'd never have time for this in med school, I had to read this author in undergraduate school. It's D. H. Lawrence."

"Correct! Roll and move again!" Jean rolled the dice and moved again to yellow - Science and Nature.

Peter looked down on the card to the question marked in yellow, "What's the most popular beverage in America?"

Maxine slapped the table and laughed so hard it was difficult for her to catch her breath, coughing so hard she had to push away from the table putting her head in her lap. "You *have got to be kidding!*"

I couldn't help myself, "Your mind always *does* take a dive into the darker side, Maxine!"

"Well hell, Honey, what the hell else could it be? It *has* to be beer!"

"Is that your answer?" Jean nodded her agreement, not wanting to take the wind out of Maxine's performance.

"Wrong. It's milk!" The entire table, except for Buck, laughed, banging the table and stomping the floor. Buck seemed somehow apprehensive at being the next to take a turn.

"See Maxine, some of our assumptions about drinking are nurtured by our need to believe them."

"Honey, who writes the damn questions for this game? It must be some ancient and feeble prohibitionist sitting in a wheelchair in some dry nursing home." Maxine drummed the table with her fingers.

"OK, Buck & Jim, your turn." Buck looked apprehensively around the table, nervously clearing his throat. Jim rolled the dice and Buck reached to move the pie shape onto the yellow, jerking his hand shakily, and trying to regain the piece and his composure, sending it rolling off the board, visibly upset with his inability to complete the task.

"It's OK, Buddy. I'll get it." Jim reached for the piece, placing it on the yellow; Buck's face reddening, his eyes darting again from player to player and nervously settling on the board.

I grabbed the card for the question, "History – Which foot did Neil Armstrong first put down on the moon?"

Jim eyed Buck noncommittally. "Any ideas, I don't have a clue."

Buck exhaled an exasperated sigh, shaking his head, and nervously grabbing his chin with his hand. "OK, OK, Armstrong stepped onto the moon with his...ah, his right foot."

"Is that your answer?"

"Yes, John, didn't you hear me? I said his right foot!"

"Sorry, Armstrong stepped with his left foot."

Buck jumped to his feet, hitting the table with his thigh and sending the game pieces flying, "Who the fuck cares? What's the point of playing this fucking game? Who in his fucking right mind cares which foot Armstrong stepped onto the moon with?"

Jim rose to put a hand on Buck's shoulder, and Buck jerked to avoid it. Jim backed away, "Buddy, it's only a game, and that's the point. We're just playing a game, trying to have a little fun." Buck grimaced; his lower lip quivering as he stormed from the kitchen and down the hall to his room, slamming the door.

We looked at each other, picking up the pieces and reassembling the board. "Jim, I'm proud of how you handled that. You were doing a nice job of trying to calm him, and you're the one who's usually so impulsive."

"I don't get it; what happened?"

"There's a therapeutic reason we encourage group activities here at Huntington; it's the same reason we have for our daily recreation therapies. How long has it been since any of us have had any fun without drinking or using before we came into treatment? What happens here is a microcosm for what life will be like on the outside. We have to learn to have fun in our recoveries. There's a lot of other things that come into play in treatment for us to begin to have that fun, and

Buck is just a little too fresh to understand most of this, or to begin trusting us and relaxing into anything enjoyable without drinking. I'm going to go see how he's doing; you guys keep playing. OK?" I left the kitchen and headed down the hall to Room 2, catching Rebecca's eye as she poked her head out of the office, nodding that I'd be OK.

I knocked softly on the paneled door. No answer. I knocked again, "Buck, can I come in?" Again, no answer; I slowly opened the door and entered. The room was cold, its window thrown open, the breeze blowing in; Buck sprawled on his back on the bed, having torn off his sweatshirt and wearing only a T shirt, arms crossed and holding onto his jumpy biceps; his cell phone lying next to him. I closed the door behind me, walked across the room and closed the window, and turned to Buck. "How're you feeling, Buddy?" I asked as softly as I could, taking the chair next to the bed. Again, silence with Buck glaring at the ceiling, his blue eyes welling with tears, his lips quivering. "Can we talk, Buck?"

"Nothing to talk about. I just called Sarah telling her I'm leaving here tonight, that I'm coming home."

"And she said what?"

A long pause, "She said that if I left I couldn't come home. Said she'd be asking for a di...divorce," Buck stammered, tears flowing freely down his face and onto the crumpled pillow.

I let him take in what he had just said, waiting for him to wipe his face with the sweatshirt he grabbed up from off the floor. Finally, I broke the silence, "All of this over a simple game, Buck; over not being able to answer a Trivial Pursuit question?"

"I'm so fucking stupid. I don't belong here with doctors and attorneys. I'm just the jock trainer who works at the gym."

"Think they knew the answer without guessing?"

Again, silence, Buck thought for a moment.

"Buck, it was just a question to guess at; nobody really knew which foot Armstrong stepped onto the moon with.

It's one of those things that don't matter, just trivia. There's something more important going on here.
What does your father do for a living?"

"He's another one of those fucking genius doctors; a fucking psychiatrist!"

"And you didn't feel like you could ever measure up."

"How, how couldn't I feel *that;* that head-shrinking fucker has been telling me I don't measure up all my life!' His words to my mother; 'That kid will never amount to anything!' He has her fucking believing it. Guess he has *me* believing it too. I went to school to do what I wanted to do, and though it's not rocket science, I've become one of the most requested personal trainers at the gym where I work. But that was never good enough for my father; if I wasn't going to be a doctor I wasn't going to be anything in his eyes."

"And Sarah, what does she think?"

"I think she went out with me because I was from what her parents called 'a good family;' because my father was a doctor. Somehow I think she measures me in my old man's shadow too."

"And so you find yourself always feeling on edge, always trying to measure up against professionals; even your wife," I reflected back. Another long pause, "Buck, one of the things we're working on here at Huntington is for you to see your value as a deserving human being. You're bright, strong, athletic, and good-looking, and I've heard your great sense of humor with Jim, when you allow your guard to fall."

Buck grimaced and shook his head in disagreement. "I thought this was about not drinking or using."

"You know, I've come to believe that only about 5% of recovery is about drinking or not drinking, using or not using; and that the other 95% is about learning to view and live life differently. You may not understand much of that right now, but if you can trust me, you will Buddy."

Buck seemed to calm, and wiped his face one last time, throwing his legs over the side of the bed and sitting up, looking at me eye to eye for the first time. "I really fucked up the game, didn't I?"

"We're all here in treatment, learning as we go. Don't you hear them out there, sounding like they're having a good time? It's just a game, Buck, and it's about us learning to enjoy ourselves without using the crutches we'd come to rely on. Want to go back?"

"I don't think I..."

"Sure you can. We'll just walk out there and take our chairs."

"Well, I, ah..."

"I thought so." I reached out my hand and after a few moments he shook it.

"Thanks John; thanks for your time. You're a decent sort of guy."

"But a bad Trivial Pursuit player; you'll see!"

We left the room, and once in the corridor could smell the heavy and intoxicating smell of perfume hanging in the air, and knew that Angel had joined the group. We took our chairs at the table. Buck looked about at the others, "Sorry everyone; just a bad night I guess."

Dave smiled and winked, "It's OK; I had a bad morning, so I guess we're even."

No surprise that Angel had pulled up a chair next to Jim, affording the group a box of expensive chocolates. Eagerly the group grabbed for the candies. It was often joked that there were four basic food groups that you'd always find in a treatment center for addictions: caffeine, nicotine, sugar and chocolate. Addiction in its simpler forms always reared its head, and because alcohol metabolizes like sugar, chocolate was usually a first choice. Buck had his original chair next to Angel, who now found herself between the two young men.

"Hmmm, this is sort of cozy, I feel like a good book nestled between two strong bookends," Angel cooed.

"Angel," I shot her a disapproving glance, taking my chair next to Dave.

"Honey, I'll bet your book has quite the story to tell," chided Maxine.

Dave broke through the sudden awkwardness, "John and I are up; we've got green for Science and Nature. You ask the question, Buck!"

Buck confidently reached in the box for the question card, "What's the most non-contagious disease in the world? And I'd *have to be asking a doctor* this!" Buck snickered, shaking his head.

Dave thought for a moment and looked to me for a clue.

"Hey, what are you looking at me for; you're the doc?"

"Non-contagious? ... hmmm, OK I'm going to guess Heart Disease."

"Is that your answer?" Buck sounded smug.

"I'd guess something else; I'd guess its *Addiction*, but some areas in Science are still having a difficult time recognizing it as a disease, even though the AMA has long recognized it as being a leading disease."

"So what's your answer," Buck smiled coyly.

"Guess I'll go with the doc's answer; Heart Disease!"

"Nope," Buck tossed the answer card in front of us, laughing. "It's *Tooth Decay*!"

"What? Tooth Decay! *Can't be*," Dave and I blurted out together, jumping to our feet in dismay and disagreement.

Buck smiled broadly, "Hey guys, *guys...* calm down; *calm down*! It's only a game!"

III

Early Gratitude

We try to celebrate holidays as best we can at Huntington. Thanksgiving is no exception, and given that Wednesday and Friday were considered normal therapeutic days of programming, those residents who lived some distance from the center, or those who were too new in treatment remained at the house during the holiday. Certainly there were visitors but residents were encouraged to celebrate at least part of the holiday as a community. It wasn't any surprise that Maxine took the lead as everyone gathered on Monday evening in the group room for the evening reflection, closing the day.

"Before we get into this evening's closing reading and our reflections…" Maxine hacked her usual cough and this time it took longer for her to regain her wind.

"Why not smoke another pack of coffin nails, Max," Dave suggested under his breath, just loud enough for her to hear.

"And Peter would have the honors of hammering them into my lid!" Maxine winked at the mortician who overheard and smiled knowingly. "As I started saying, I'd be willing to orchestrate a Thanksgiving Dinner here, if anyone's interested."

"What, you're going to shove a turkey in the microwave?" I questioned, taking my seat within the circle. "We don't have a regular oven."

"No, John! Do you think *I'd* know how to cook a bird," Maxine cackled and coughed. "The only way I'd know if the damn turkey was done is if I'd stuffed it with popcorn, turned up the heat, and wait for it's ass to blow off!" It got the laugh she wanted.

"Maxine!" I cautioned with my disapproving look, but as usual she dismissed me.

"There's a caterer near here who'd deliver the bird and all the trimmings. I found his ad in this morning's paper." She looked around the circle. "Anybody interested? We'd pass the hat, collect the money and we could still pick up those other things that make Thanksgiving what we remember it or want it to be."

"I think it's a really great idea," I supported her suggestion.

"But I spent the day drinking as much as I could, starting as early as I could," Jim blurted out, winking at Maxine who rolled her eyes, trying to ignore him.

"Well, maybe we could start a *new tradition* for ourselves and right here at Huntington?"

Maxine looked as though I had lost my mind. "And have Thanksgiving here *every year*? I don't think so." Maxine laughed and coughed so long and hard we thought she wouldn't catch her breath. "I'm still trying to get my ass out of here before the Christmas tree goes up, or maybe your thinking I'll be the damn angel at the top, with the tree shoved up my…"

"*Maxine!*" I stopped her short with a more demanding look of disapproval. "More of that and we'll have you coloring eggs too!"

"Over my trampled, dead and buried body!"

Peter nodded his head with an accommodating smile, getting *his* laugh from the group.

"No Maxine, you know what I mean. We'd start our tradition of enjoying any holiday without drinking or using."

Buck rolled his eyes, shaking his head. "I don't know guys, it sounds a little disappointing."

"I know Buck, I know. When I was in treatment I didn't know how I'd ever enjoy a holiday again. But wait and see. You might surprise yourself." Buck bit his lip and shrugged his resignation.

Jean, sitting next to Buck, who had been at the treatment center the longest and who was looking at discharging in a couple of weeks, slapped Buck's knee. "You might find you'll have more to be grateful for than you might imagine."

Thanksgiving arrived, and many of the residents slept in until we gathered at 10 AM for a late holiday meditation to begin our day, while the early risers watched The Macy's Parade broadcast from New York, featuring this year's version of a monstrous "Mickey" gliding past the skyscrapers like an impotent and captive version of King Kong.

It was a cold though quiet morning with large flakes of snow in the air, and being a week day I found myself working, with my family planning an evening celebration at home. I didn't mind working this holiday, as everything I had come to feel grateful for originated during my own days in treatment at Huntington.

The morning meditation was short, with our reflecting merely on the reading of the day, with me suggesting we'd all consider our gratitude in a simple prayer of thanksgiving as we sat down to a treatment center feast. Angel arrived late in her short bathrobe, as hot a shade of pink as her spaghetti-strapped top. Reluctantly I had to excuse her from the group, telling her again how inappropriate it was to present herself at meditation dressed as she was.

The residents had invited me to join the banquet at noon and I questioned being stuffed twice before the day ended. Reluctantly, I told myself, I needed to join them yet not really believing anything I was trying to rationalize about my true motives. The house began to take on a holiday feel. It was something more than the anticipation of a meal that was better than hospital food. It had something to do with gathering around a common warmth we all sensed rising within us; some more than others.

Although breaking every fire code, I allowed a couple of safely situated candles to be burning in the kitchen and dining room; their *Pumpkin Spice* and *Cinnamon Apple* scents permeating the first floor, warming Dave as he returned from picking up the pumpkin and sweet potato pies he had ordered from the bakery promising to remain open until noon. He was dressed in a sport coat and tie, and caught me shaking my head and smiling as he passed the office door with the delicacies.

"What? You don't like pumpkin or sweet potato?"

"It's not the pies, Dave. You sure you want to dress *that well* here at the center? You're not in your office seeing patients!"

He looked embarrassed. "That's what Max said, but I don't know that I've ever seen her in a dress, so I didn't…"

"I think most everyone is going to be fairly laid back today."

"OK, I catch your drift…I'll find my jeans. Actually it'll feel good to kick back on a holiday for once. They're always so formal at our house."

Buck, in his dark hooded sweat suit had run out as well, saying he had promised to get cigarettes for Maxine and upon his return fumbled with a bouquet of rust and gold gas station flowers, asking a bit uneasily if we had a vase hidden under the office sink.

"Maybe I should *check those* first," I toyed with him. "No telling what you could be bringing in."

His face reddened, Buck winked my way. "Just a *fucking* vase, John; I don't need an editorial!"

"OK! OK," I threw up my arms in submission, "One vase for the Flower Boy, coming up!"

Buck laughed and grabbed it from me, pausing before heading down the hallway, "You know; this may not be so bad after all."

"That's because you're realizing *you're* not so bad after all!"

If Buck had paused, he was now stopped dead in his tracks, his eyes welling with tears he quickly brushed aside with the back of his free hand. "I couldn't be doing this if is hadn't been for you, John." Buck pointed to the office chair. "You believed in me right from the beginning, when I threw my attitude into that chair the day I arrived."

I felt the emotion too. "Buck, I had people believing in me when I first got here. Continuing recovery is a *We* Program. It's about *all of us* together. We need to continue believing in each other and allowing ourselves the strength of the recovering fellowship; accepting it when we need it, affording it to others when they need it. It's about all of us together."

"Happy Thanksgiving, John," Buck stretched out his hand.

I took it and pulled him close and into a hug, "Happy Thanksgiving!" As he turned to leave, I caught myself asking, "Hey, I almost forgot; have you seen Jim this morning? He didn't make it to morning meditation."

"Must have overslept – want me to go up and check on him…make sure he's up?"

"I've got to get some things out of the hall closet up there anyway, I'll check his room."

Buck continued out the door, pausing again. "Thanks again, John. I'm glad it was you who admitted me to Huntington. I don't think I'd have stayed otherwise."

"What, you'd have *gone back out there* and lost everything?"

Buck thought a moment. "You just made it easier. It's a bitch when you find yourself checking into a treatment center, finding yourself being forced to your knees."

I knew how he felt, remembering my own first minutes at Huntington, and as I felt myself again quickly becoming more serious, I also sensed an opportunity, "*But are you*, are you on your knees, Buck?"

"What do you…?"

"Do you understand and *feel* that you don't have any control over alcohol or drugs?"

"It's the *First Step* that we keep talking about, isn't it? How we recognize that we don't have any control over alcohol or…"

"I *know* Buck. But do you *feel* it? It's one thing to understand it intellectually, but do you truly *feel* it?" I slapped my chest, "In here…do you feel it in here? Do you understand that you can *never* drink again?"

Buck grew silent; his broad shoulders sank. He moved back into the office and closed the door, resting himself against the back of it, looking deep into me. "I know this doesn't make any sense, but I've been thinking about it a lot lately. I know I can't drink. It doesn't take a genius to figure it out. I almost lost everything and especially Sarah, and I know how the cravings work, drawing me back into my old ways of thinking. I think I'm getting it, John, but…" Buck paused.

"But?" I could feel his struggle and confusion.

"But, I've got such a fucking hard time believing *I can never drink again!*" Buck searched my face, hoping I'd have the answer, hoping I wouldn't think him the idiot for suggesting something so preposterous.

"I know." I caught myself reaching back. "I know. I felt exactly the same way, and I was a lot older than you are now. Buck I have to believe it's that much more difficult for you, being 28 and you're finding yourself feeling the party's over. It's easy for me suggesting at my age that your party's *just beginning*…and though that may sound like bullshit, given where the alcohol will take you *if you do go back out there,* your party truly *is* just beginning."

Buck nodded knowingly, "But…but *never* again! Something's changed. The playing field isn't the same. I can't play the game like the others anymore. Something about me is different."

"I know; it's different for millions of us, and what you suggest is exactly what we need to do - *learn to play the game differently*! It's why we're here in treatment."

Buck looked at me as though I had just had a stroke, trying to understand, "In treatment to learn to play the game differently?"

"I think that only about 5% of our recovery concerns drinking or not drinking – using or not using, and that the other 95% regards our learning to live life differently."

"I guess I begin to..."

I interrupted, "Learning to live life on life's terms, not avoiding or running from, and breaking through the illusions we were either taught or build around ourselves." I paused, "Sorry I cut you off, I didn't mean to..."

"You really believe in recovery, don't you, John."

"It means *everything* to me."

"'Never again', and 'the party's over?'"

"The party's *just* beginning. I know that's hard to swallow, but for now will you just trust me when I tell you that as we move on in working The 12 Steps we begin to see things differently, and that it gets easier?"

Buck paused, looking deeply into me, "If there's one thing I've learned it's that I can trust you, John. All of this isn't easy for me, and I don't fully know what it is about you, but I *do* trust you."

"Thanks Buck! And in the Second and Third Steps we'll begin trusting in something much higher than either one of us."

Buck exhaled deeply, grabbed his flowers, turned and opened the door. I followed and as he headed toward the kitchen I took the stairs to wake up Jim, stopping at the closet across the hall from his room and fumbling with my keys to open the door.

"Hey, who's...," I heard the startled and muffled words coming from Jim's room.

I turned away from the closet and knocking on his door, there was no response except for the rustling of bedclothes. "Jim, you awake?" Again, no response, "Jim, it's John; you missed the morning meditation." No response, except for more rustling and a hushed whisper. As my heart sank it quickened, "Jim, I'm going to have to open…" There was more rustling and still no response. I turned the doorknob, pushing the door open.

"No, no don't," came Jim's words as he sat up in bed, pulling the comforter over him as Angel tightened the sheets around herself. "No, John, don't…"

Without thinking, I entered the room, pushing aside Angels pink robe lying at the entrance. I felt my anger rise and my face redden. "I'm going to leave this room as quickly as I entered. Angel, I want you out of here as soon as I leave." Picking up the pink robe I tossed it to her.

"John, it's not what you…" Angel started.

"*Not what I think?* Is that what you're going to say?" She became silent, smirking a 'who cares anyway' look my way. Jim nervously fidgeted with the bedcovers, pulling them even closer. "I want you out of this room, and I want you dressed *appropriately* and in the office in 15 minutes. Jim, I want you in the office in half an hour, and I suggest each of you bring your resident handbooks with you, open to the section regarding 'rules and expectations." I turned and pulled the door shut behind me.

Maxine, within earshot and passing me in the hall, paused in her lumberjack plaid shirt and fluffy slippers, "You *have got to be kidding!*"

I shot her a harried glance, "Addiction, in all its ugly forms!" and headed down the stairs.

Fifteen, twenty, twenty-five minutes passed, as I anxiously waited, knowing what needed to be done. Angel didn't appear. Suddenly I could hear the thud of luggage being pulled down the stairwell and into the hallway leading past the office. Dave was heading to the office as Angel rolled her bags past him, her coat on and pink boa wrapped around her neck. "Where are *you* headed, Angel? Get a late pass to go home?" Angel ignored him as she did me, heading for the door.

"Angel, we need to talk."

"I'm out of here," was her emphatic reply, not affording me a glance.

"Angel, if you're leaving, there's some paperwork that needs…"

"Fuck the paperwork! Fuck this god-damned hole." Angel reached the door, grabbed the knob and kicking the door open pushed through it, pulling her belongings behind her, her boa catching in the door as it slammed in the wind. Not turning to retrieve it, she raged a string of expletives all the way to the parking lot.

Dave looked to me for an explanation, "What? She doesn't like turkey?" Jim entered the hallway, and Dave catching the look in his eye as he headed for the office, passed him, deciding it best to come back later.

Jim dressed in his jeans and a simple sweater sheepishly entered the office, carrying the treatment center handbook and slowly closing the door behind him and taking a chair. Not saying a word he looked beyond me and out the windows at the huge flakes of snow falling onto the last leaves of autumn that blanketed the lawn, his hands nervously fidgeting at the arms of the chair.

"So, you and Angel had this planned?" my voice giving away the anger and disappointment I was feeling. "You don't come down for morning meditation, and she dresses in a way that she knows will get her sent out of the group – and while we're occupied you two are together in your room?"

"It didn't happen that way," Jim suggested meekly, again growing silent and continuing to look beyond me.

Moments passed before I continued. "Well, how *did* it happen?"

Jim looked at me for the first time and after a long pause, "What damned difference does it make, John?" He took his handbook and pushed it across the desk. "I'm out of here anyway. It's all there in the rules, 'Any sexual contact is immediate grounds for dis…dismissal from the program." Jim's emotions began to take over, and leaning forward put his face in his hands, and looking at the floor continued, "I'm not ready. I can't go out there and…"

"Then *why* would you put yourself in a situation that…"

"Put *myself* in a situation?" Jim looked up at me, continuing to hold his head. "I didn't put myself in *any* situation! And I'd *never* intentionally fall for any woman's…" " Jim stopped short of going further, almost as if he was affording too wide an opening into himself.

"What?"

"You know I don't miss meditation, John."

"I know, and this morning you decide that there's something, or should I say *somebody* more important than…"

"John, hold on. I forgot to set my fucking alarm, and you know how hard it is for me to get up in the first place."

"Are you trying to tell me that…"

"You're going to believe what you want, but I'm telling you I wasn't in meditation because I overslept."

"What about Angel?"

"You're a human being, a guy. What would you do if you woke up and found – hell, what do I mean *found?* What if you *felt and smelled the warmth of another body*…" Jim looked at me, and reworded his answer. "Look, I woke up and slowly, to a warm body under my covers inching its' way closer next to me."

I looked at him incredulously.

"And the rest is history." Again, Jim's eyes avoided mine and searched the floor for anything more that needed saying. Nothing came.

I walked over to the windows looking out, not knowing what to say; not exactly believing the rules entirely applied to the situation Jim was presenting me. The snow had stopped, and the dark clouds seemed to be parting to where one might just be able to hope for a glimmer of sunlight. "So, where do you think this leaves you?"

Jim cautiously responded, "John, I don't think I stand a prayer. Dr. Segen and Gerry will have my ass out of here just as soon as you make the calls, won't they?"

I couldn't answer immediately, continuing my gaze out the window. Finally, "I don't know Jim; this doesn't look good. It sends a bad message through the rest of the house."

"Yup, I thought so. I'll start getting my things together and…"

"Do you *want* to stay?"

Jim looked incredulous, and with a ray of excitement in his voice, "John, you don't think that…"

"I don't know. I can't speak for either Dr. Segen or Gerry." I faced him and paused, "But I know how much you want this, Jim. I remember how you returned from pass because you thought you were too impulsive to stay *out there* for the weekend, that you couldn't resist the cravings you were having, and I know how much you've been trying to help Buck, and I can see how…"

Jim was on his feet, "John, you don't really think that…?"

"I don't know. I'll have to call both the doc and therapist. It's their call, but I will tell them what I think, if they ask."

Jim put out his hand, and I shook it. "I can't ask for more than that."

"I should have a good feel for this in about half an hour. Until then, what are you going to tell the group?"

"Hadn't thought I'd need to do that. What do you think?"

"I guess I'd tell them the truth, but trust me, don't try to put any sort of *macho guy spin* to the story, or your butt will be.…"

"I won't, John. Trust me, there's not a *guy spin* to spin, and…" Again Jim stopped short nervously avoiding my eyes, finding me thinking he wanted to tell me more, as if there was a something that would convince me even more. Again he avoided it.

"You might mention that you're hoping against hope that given the circumstances you might have a leg to stand on. My guess is that you'll find most of them in the kitchen. I'll get you back in the office when I know more."

"I don't know how I can thank you for standing behind me."

"Jim, we're not *out of the woods* yet. However this turns out; just know we need to learn that when we give up one addiction it's easy to pick up another. Sometimes we can't see it coming, like we couldn't see our other addictions presenting themselves."

Jim left the office, reluctantly heading for the others. I could hear Maxine on him before he even got into the kitchen, "What the hell were you doing with Angel in you…"

Buck was on him too. "Doesn't your treatment mean *anything* to you? You have to be fucking crazy to…"

I could barely hear Jim's sheepish reply, "Hey guys, can we just sit and talk about…?" I could hear chairs being pulled to the kitchen table.

My heart sank as I closed the office door, preparing myself to make the calls I'd have to make and for the questions that would have to be answered. Gerry and Dr. Segen knew better than I did, and I'd have to trust in their decision. I picked up the phone.

The caterer arrived with the feast. Buck had found the extra leaf for the kitchen table and while both he and Jim tried figuring out how to set a table, Peter and Dave carved the turkey as Maxine and Jean found bowls for the dressing, sweet potatoes, mashed potatoes, gravy and cranberries.

I opened the office door, walked down the hallway and motioned to an anxious Jim to return to the office. "Good luck, man," Buck suggested as Jim followed me into the office. Jim was allowed to remain in treatment though was restricted to the house, having lost his privileges for the coming week. He was to meet with both the therapist and doctor the next morning and they were to discuss the incident further.

As he was leaving the office, elated and ready to join the group, he turned back to me, "John, it's because of what you said, isn't it?"

"No Jim. It's because of a lot of things, but mostly it's because of how much you want your recovery." Jim couldn't say anything. With his eyes remaining focused on mine, he just nodded, knowingly.

Finally we all sat down at the kitchen table, the smells of Thanksgiving permeating the room whetting our appetites. Jean dressed in a festive but comfortable autumn sweatshirt had taped the full front page – the morning newspaper illustration to the cupboard. It was Norman Rockwell's 1940s painting, 'Freedom From Want' celebrating the holiday, with the newspaper caption in bold letters, 'We Give Thanks.'

I asked for us to consider what we had to be grateful for, and as we went around the table each of us talked about our sobriety, or new found freedom from the use of drugs. We were grateful we were alive and feeling better, both about ourselves and life in general. Jim added, "I'm grateful that I can continue in treatment." We all felt good about him being able to remain with us, and Jean suggested she hoped that Angel would find her way into another form of treatment.

As Dave, looking so comfortable in his worn Notre Dame shirt and Levis passed the platter of turkey, Buck pointed to the Rockwell painting, finding us all following his lead, "Do you think there ever was a Thanksgiving celebration as happy as that?" We considered the front page painting, featuring 11 family members of all ages gathered around grandma bringing in the huge turkey, celebrating the feast in front of them; all smiling and ecstatic.

"Sure was never like that at our house when I was growing up," Jim offered. "When my family gathered around a Thanksgiving table it wouldn't be 10 minutes before some argument started. Liquor was always flowing before the meal and there was always enough wine being poured to keep *the buzz* going. My old man would always get into something with one of us kids, get pissed and before we were finished eating he'd storm off into the family room where he'd pour himself another *stiff one*, pout and finally fall asleep. After a couple of years we'd push to start the argument earlier just to get him off the table."

Peter grabbed the huge turkey leg on his plate, and trying to excuse his using his hands as if it were a simple chicken leg, continued the conversation. "Not at our house. You'd never catch me in my sweat suit," he motioned to the comfortable and worn UW sweats he was wearing. "My wife made sure of that. She'd start in on me the night before, lecturing about how much work the day was for her and how I dare not ruin it by getting loaded. She'd set the perfect table, down to the silver napkin holders, and nervously coached the kids on drinking from her blessed Waterford crystal glasses. You'd never catch me grabbing a drumstick like this," he suggested, waving it emphatically over his head, "or she'd cut me off from any of her blessed favors until Christmas, and then only if I got lucky!" His anger was rising, as he dropped the leg back onto his plate with a thud.

Maxine coughed, her cigarette pack nearly falling out of her lumberjack shirt, and leaned across the table almost knocking over her Styrofoam cup of water, mimicking Gerry conducting group "So, how do you *really* feel? You know, *down deep?*" She got her expected laugh and Peter relaxed. "How'd you make it through the day without the booze?" she continued.

"Well, we're a creative lot, aren't we Max?" He winked at Maxine and looked around the table, asking that the dressing be passed, and getting a few knowing nods, went on. "If I was lucky, I'd plan my week as much as possible and have some work to do later in the day to coincide with when we were done with dinner. If I was really lucky on Thanksgiving I'd have my *Bertha* or *Bruno* downstairs who needed attending; you know, some final touches for the next days showing!"

"Thank God for Bertha and Bruno," Maxine coughed, pointing to the Rockwell painting, "And Grandpa standing behind Grandma holding the turkey probably can't wait to get into his own embalming fluid!"

"Yup, you've got it right Max; some late afternoon FM Christmas tunes opening the holiday season, the company of a Bertha or Bruno, and my bottle of vodka from the embalming fluid cupboard. My wife finally guessed what was happening, on that particular Thanksgiving evening when she caught me in a bad lipstick mishap, mistaking a Bruno for a Bertha. She actually saved my ass, before the visitation started, though never let me forget it."

"You have *got to be* kidding! You're making that one up."

"Wish I were."

Jean put down her fork, "Any *other* great Thanksgiving stories? How about we hold off on some of the less pleasant shop talk for tomorrow's group?"

"Sorry Jean," Peter moved his attention to Buck, who had hardly touched anything on his plate, "And what about you, Flower Boy? You're sure the quiet one today."

Buck looked nervously around the table, more anxious than usual. "It's nothing," he fidgeted with his silverware, glancing over to me and then looking away, silence filling the room.

I began slowly, remembering the Trivial Pursuit situation and how Buck finds it difficult being singled out. "Buck, you may find things difficult to talk about, but Buddy, it's not *nothing*. We can go somewhere else for *a breather* if you'd feel more comfortable..."

"It's really noth...well, it *is* something." Buck took a look at the painting and shook his head slowly. "That painting has been lying to us since World War II, having us believe that there *really are* families like that. I...I'm just having a hard time..." Buck grew silent again.

Jim impulsively jumped in, "What is it Buck? Come on; look at the support you gave me this morning. Can't we offer you…"

Buck began slowly, "My wife called. She's coming to visit this afternoon; said she'd like to spend some time with me. I don't know if I'm ready to…"

"How bad can it be? She *wants* to spend time with you."

I felt the need to jump in. "Buck, if you don't feel you can handle…"

"Oh, it's not that. I guess I'm not sure I'm ready to tell her what I think we should do with our marriage. I'm not sure *how* I feel. We've been talking about separating."

"Then maybe you need to tell her exactly that, that you're unsure."

"But I'm never unsure of anything when it comes to her."

"What? It would sound *unmanly* not to be sure?"

Buck's eyes darted around the table, and suddenly I felt I'd pushed too far. He returned his focus on me. "I guess that might be the…"

"She might welcome that kind of vulnerability, that kind of honesty."

Dave, who had been silent to this point, began slowly, "Buck, if there's one thing I've learned about my wife and our relationship, it's that there's nothing more intimate or attractive to a spouse who's been lied to than *honesty*. And if there's one thing that might top even that, especially for a wife who's had to deal with a macho and dishonest husband, it's his sense of vulnerability when the chips are down, and the opening he affords her to finally help him." The room remained silent for a long moment, but it wasn't uncomfortable, not even for Buck whose blue eyes looked thoughtfully into his plate of food.

Buck picked up his fork and began to play with his mashed potatoes, like some kid needing to be coaxed into eating, and feeling as much suggested, "Guess it's true about recovery. In the beginning a guy starts by taking *baby steps*."

I reached for another slice of white meat, pausing in my reach "And together we learn to walk, and together we learn to fly."

Again, silence filled the room until Jim blew a hole in it. "F…fuck Rockwell's fantasies," Jim stammered, pointing to the painting with his knife, "I wouldn't trade this Thanksgiving table for that one, *any* day! God bless us all!" It was perfect, with everyone clapping and meeting Jim's poignant blessing with unabashed approval. Buck suddenly found his appetite and the meal continued, a bit lighter and more joyous until everyone had had their fill and pushed back from the table.

"So let's start cutting into those pies that Dave brought in this morning?" Maxine hacked, clearing her throat as she pushed her own chair back, getting to her feet. "I'll get them!" She headed to the kitchen counter, pulling the Rockwell print off the cupboard in passing, crumpling it and tossing it into the trash, suggesting, "We sure do know how to throw a better party!"

Buck eyed me across the table, suggesting to everyone, "I've got so very much to be thankful for."

"We all do Buck, we all do, Buddy!"

IV

Darkness Before Dawn

November quickly fell off into December as the barren and overcast landscape resigned itself to both freezing temperatures and the mounting snow that blanketed the dormant flower gardens outside the office windows. Jim had his restriction lifted and was on a regular schedule, though cautioned that any further *fraternizing* with the opposite sex would not be tolerated and he'd have to leave. He suggested he had learned a great deal about his impulsivity and cross addictions and seemed truly grateful for being allowed to remain at Huntington. He had made it his recent mission to try to pull Buck out of a funk he had obviously fallen into. Buck just wasn't the same, seeming more anxious and *out of sorts* than was usual.

It was a Friday morning and I was happy to be looking forward to my weekend off. Dr. Segen had just seen Buck in his office across from mine and when leaving I could hear him tell the doctor he'd find Maxine for him. Passing my door he asked if I knew where Max was, looking more perplexed and preoccupied about his own concerns than about Maxine's whereabouts.

"She's working on her *Fourth Step* Inventory in the lounge. Just follow the sounds of her coughing." Buck continued to look preoccupied with his own thoughts and not quite with what I was saying about Maxine. "You doing OK, Buddy?"

"I guess so. It's just not an easy time for me. I said it was OK for Dr. Segen to talk with my old...ah, my father. He did and we were talking about how he's beginning to see the light."

"And you're not sure about that?"

Buck looked at me helplessly. "I don't know if I know the guy Segen's talking with or about! My old man *seeing the light?* You've got to be shittin' me! Sure doesn't sound like my *shrink* father." From across the hall we could hear Dr. Segen rolling his chair back from the desk where he was writing a progress note in Buck's chart. Buck turned toward the open door behind him, "Doc, I'm on my way. Max is right down the hall."

As Buck headed out, Dr. Segen came into the office and returned Buck's chart to the rack as he pulled out Maxine's. He looked my way, "Buck has a lot on his plate right now, trying to make a decision with Sarah about their relationship, struggling with his *Second and Third Steps*, and now his father enters the picture and is trying to rebuild a relationship; making up for lost time - almost as if he wants his psychiatric cut in his son's recovery. He called me and wants to send over a minister who he thinks might help with his son's spiritual needs." He put the chart under his arm and replenished his coffee from the pot on the counter, eyeing me cautiously. "He could hardly say the word *spiritual* – had to spit it out; as if it went against everything he did and didn't believe in. Still, he's smart enough to know his son would only view his professional efforts as pure mechanical posturing, and that he shouldn't be *working that territory* with his son anyway. Although I'll bet he continues to try."

"So, what do you think?"

"As a psychiatrist I think the father has a blind spot for his son. I told Buck to go slowly, that even though his fathers' efforts might seem sincere this was his recovery and not his father's." Juggling the chart and coffee and heading out the door, hearing Maxine's cough drawing closer, "How's Maxine been? She said she wants to see me for some decongestants and sleep meds; that her cough has been getting worse, that she's been coughing up blood?"

"She didn't mention anything about blood to me, but I sure wish she'd give up the smoking."

"One thing at a time John; I'm with you, but we've got to make certain her recovery is well underway before she attacks that. I'll talk to her about it." He headed for his office as his next patient met him. "How are you doing, Maxine?"

She looked drawn and worn as she entered the office, reaching for the arm of the chair to steady herself, coughing violently, "I need something, something for this god forsaken cough." The doctor closed the door as I reached for the phone, ringing for attention.

"Huntington House, John speaking."

"Hello, this is Pastor William Burnum. I need to speak with
Dr. Jaeger's son, Robert. Is he there?"

The voice sounded officious to the point of being rude. I wanted to say, *'you mean Buck,'* but remembered our rules regarding patient confidentiality, and knew Buck had only signed to receive calls from his wife, parents and a few friends. "I'm sorry Pastor, but given our rules regarding confidentiality, I'm unable to acknowledge that we have a resident by that name. I can take your name and if he's a resident can have him return the call." I tried being as pleasant as I could, knowing how clumsy I sounded.

The voice was impatient and escalated in intensity, "Look, let's not play games. Just get Robert for me!"

I tried remaining calm, "I'm sorry Pastor, but you can understand that patient confidentiality is one of our highest concerns, and if a resident hasn't signed to..."

"That's ridiculous and there are exceptions to all rules, especially when you're talking with a minister who..."

I lost my patience, "Look Pastor, I'm sorry, but...

"But nothing; I'll have his father call him to sign a god damned..." He caught himself and paused, "... I'll *have a word* with his father about how you people deal with the *true* professionals trying to help these people who've fallen into moral decay." He slammed the receiver.

Moral decay - it was how the majority of society continued to view alcoholism and the other addictions. I felt my anger rising and was glad to have him off the phone, thinking how that sort of self-righteous religiosity and morality kept recovering people mired in their guilt and remorse. I was hoping that Buck's father, being an MD might afford himself the more medically knowledgeable model for alcoholism and addiction – that it's a disease. I had my doubts.

The door across the hall opened, and Dr. Segen pulling a stethoscope from around his neck stuck his head in the office, "John, call the ER at the general hospital downtown and see if you can get a driver to take Max there. I'm ordering an X-ray of her lungs. I just want to make certain she doesn't have pneumonia, and there's the blood thing. I just don't like it. I took her vitals and she's running a low grade temp and her lungs really don't sound good."

"You bet!" I got on the phone and made the necessary calls, and within the hour we had Max on her way, fussing and fuming about just needing cough medicine.

Gerry stopped to see Dr. Segen before he left, and to grab coffee on his way downstairs to lead the morning group. I told him about Maxine being sent to ER. He was concerned, and on his way out of the office asked if I had heard the weather report. We were in for some heavy snow, the first real storm of the season, and I was grateful I had driven my Chevy Blazer with its four wheel drive, no matter how old it was.

Stopping on his way downstairs Buck asked to sign the release saying he could receive calls from Reverend Burnum. I questioned him cautiously, "Do you know him Buck?"

"Haven't met him, but my father called saying he might be good for me. I called him and gave him my cell phone number, but just in case he calls on the office phone, you can talk with him. Guess my father's trying to make an effort to help."

"With a minister?"

"He knows his head-shrinking isn't going to get him very far, and besides I guess I could use some help on my Second and Third Steps."

I eyed Buck cautiously, and he caught my concern, "Just remember that religion and spirituality don't always shake out to being the same thing."

"I think I know what you mean, John."

I looked at the broad-shouldered rock-of-a-man standing in front of me, "You're still very fragile in your recovery, Buck; you've had a lot to think about lately. And now I sense you wanting to please your father – it might be too much of a bite to chew."

"Dr. Segen said pretty much the same thing. I *will* go slowly, but I've agreed to meet him tonight. He's coming to see me after the AA Meeting, about 8 o'clock."

"OK Buddy, I'll tell the PM people to expect him." I checked the clock, "Hey, better get your butt downstairs; you don't want to be late for Gerry's group!"

After lunch the general hospital phoned asking for Dr. Segen. I paged him and had him return the call to the ER. He called back telling us that Maxine was being kept for observation and that she was going to have more X-rays and tests; that she was to be seen by an oncologist who was being called in. "John, it doesn't look good for her," he suggested, with more concern than I had heard in his voice in a long time.

"Cancer?"

"They're waiting for the oncologist to make that call, but the ER doc tells me that both lungs look bad."

My heart sank as I held my breath. "How can she make it though treatment?"

"Let's wait before we start jumping any guns, John; time for a few prayers, and taking this one step in front of the other, and one day at a time."

As I was giving the shift turnover to Dale and Rebecca the phone rang. The hacking cough told me immediately it was Maxine. There was a pause and without her usual brash gusto, slowly stated, "I've...I've got lung cancer."

I paused, gathering my words slowly and feeling each one of them, "I'm sorry Max. I'm *so* sorry, but there are such miraculous cures in Medicine these days."

Again, there was a long pause and only then did she slowly continue, "How the hell am I going to get through this without drinking?"

I felt the pain, felt every syllable of the sobering question being asked. Moments passed, listening to her labored breathing through the receiver. "Max," I began softly and deliberately, tears welling up in my eyes, "how would you get through this *if you were* drinking?"

I tried to leave my work at the treatment center for the weekend, heading home to write Christmas cards, and helping with the decorations; trying to keep up with the snow – shoveling the drive and walk again and again. It's a funny thing about Christmas. During my drinking days it was my most celebrated holiday, trying to find meaning in the season, and sharing in the relationships of both family and friends. In my mind it had to be the *perfect* holiday, down to coordinated lights, decorations, wrapping paper and bows; all recorded in the perfect photos and videos. I would always take vacation days and the liquor cabinet was always stocked and restocked. Although everything looked perfect and people viewed us as the perfect family, I felt empty and tried desperately to live in the illusions of a brandy-induced fog; in images of holidays past and the warming Christmas tree lit fantasies of what the holidays present could never be. By the time New Years' morning came I was glad to be rid of it all, exhausted in the stupor afforded by the night before and the shattered dreams of what Christmas again didn't provide me. How empty I would feel, beginning to drink even more to repress the feelings. And now things are simpler; a simple tree, a warming fire in the hearth, a few cards to friends, and the warmth of family. Yet even now, after my own accumulated years of sobriety I remain the most cautious during the holiday season, as I remember how easy it was for me to fall into the materialistic alcohol-advertised-glow of the merchant's favorite season.

On Sunday my wife and I journeyed out in the snow after the storm had past; a white countryside bathed in sunlight to visit Maxine at the hospital. Max looked tired and worn in her hospital bed; not the unsinkable Molly Brown-of-a-force to be reckoned with that she always postured at the house.

Placing a vase of yellow roses on her table, I introduced her to Joanne, "How are you feeling, Max?"

"Never guessed this'd happen to me," she coughed the words. "Should have though, with the way I smoked." Her hair was drawn back and she spoke nervously about her new crisis. She was being given oxygen and said she'd be bringing it with her when she returned to treatment. She wanted to complete her work at Huntington. "Got to keep fighting, but I'm not sure which is worse – alcoholism or this?

I took her hand as Joanne stood by me, "Guess this is the perfect time to practice your surrender, Max?"

"You really believe that don't you?" Maxine coughed so hard I wasn't certain she could rally back into normal breathing, dislodging the tubes from her nose. Repositioning the oxygen with shaky hands, "It's so damn hard; I was never about to surrender to anything – so god damned un-American! I wasn't going to give up my will to anyone or anything!"

Rubbing her hand gently, "I felt the same way, until an old timer made it easier for me. He said it wasn't so much a giving up of the will as it was *an opening* of the will."

She hacked another sustained cough, "Semantics, just semantics!"

I remained silent for the moment, collecting my thoughts, "Wasn't for me; it was exactly what I needed. I needed to open myself to enough humility to just begin to appreciate that I didn't know everything there is to know – that there were possibilities I couldn't fully comprehend, that I could never fully understand…that…"

"Humility was never *my* middle name!"

"It wasn't mine either!" Joanne nodded all too quickly, and I gave her an affectionate elbow in the ribs.

Max coughed and sighed, "Always thought I could handle anything; God was always out there and unapproachable."

"Maybe *you* were unapproachable." Maxine fell quiet, searching the ceiling with her dark eyes. "Max, again it was one of the old timers in recovery who suggested to me, '*The only thing you initially need to know about God is that you're not it!*' That I could buy into, and that was enough humility – just a seed, to begin my journey into surrendering my struggle, surrendering my powerlessness."

"Over alcohol," Maxine coughed again, "But what about…"

"Over *anything* I found myself powerless over. Recovery isn't just about drinking or not drinking – it's about how we approach life in all of the ways it presents itself."

Maxine raised her head looking deeply into me, "You have got to be kidding. Cancer, John? What do you know about cancer?"

Suddenly I felt helpless. What *did* I now about cancer? Holding her hand, I suddenly found myself squeezing it. The room fell silent and again moments passed. My helplessness continued, "Maybe you'll teach me, Max. Maybe there's a lot you can teach me."

Monday morning came early and as I climbed the treatment center steps to the front door in the early morning dawn Buck was there to meet me. "Hey, what are you doing up so early?"

"Thought I could buy you coffee this morning."

"Are we selling the stuff now?"

Buck smiled nervously, "Thought you'd have a few minutes for me after you take turnover from the night shift."

"Sure I will, Buddy; any word about Maxine?"

"They're starting a course of chemo right away. Her family wanted to move her home, but she wants to stay here and finish her treatment and remain close to the doctors she now has."

"She's back here in the house?" It seemed impossible.

"Not yet today; they want to begin the treatments and see how it goes."

"She's a fighter. I'll give her that! I'll bet she *is* back in the house before long."

"So, we'll have coffee?"

"Make a strong pot!"

"Two strong coffees coming up, I'll meet you in the lounge." Buck was on his way down the hall as I entered the office. Turnover was short and the house was quiet. In fifteen minutes I was on my way down the hall, following the smell of fresh coffee and stopping to say good morning to Peter, passing me.

"You're up early, just like Buck; ready for another week of it!"

"It's always good to find ourselves on this side of the grave."

"Guess you'd know about that!"

"I'm thinking that recovery will keep me on this earth longer."

"And your living life more fully."

"I'm beginning to get a feel for that John, and I've been thinking...thinking about leaving the funeral business."

I thought for a moment, "Maybe not a bad idea. Why not take that into group and get some feedback?"

I left Peter to consider it as he went into the TV Room to watch the morning news and I walked into the lounge; Buck in his Levis and slate blue cotton sweater, sitting at the table in front of the windows and watching the sun come up over the snow covered landscape – two steaming mugs of coffee in front of him. Hearing me enter he pointed out the window, "Do you see the white-tailed doe walking through the garden. She stopped and looked straight at me. It's wonderful isn't it?"

It was a beautiful sight, the graceful animal comfortable in her surroundings, "And if this were two months ago you'd be waking up to a painfully heavy head and wondering what you said or did last night."

"Yup, and now I wake up, excited about what the day might bring."

"Just another miracle, Buck; just another simple and quiet miracle afforded us at the dawn of another day in our continuing recoveries." I took the chair across the table from him, Buck pushing my mug of coffee in front of me.

"Thanks for spending a few minutes with me."

"What's up?"

Buck eyed me cautiously, "I'm leaving Huntington today."

I picked up my coffee, feeling my heart sink. "Buck, I don't know that you're..."

"It was a long weekend, John," Buck was nervous and began fidgeting in his chair. "I had a long visit with Sarah on Saturday, after spending an even longer Friday night with Pastor Burnum. And all of a sudden my father thinks he's my oldest friend."

"And that makes you think you're ready to leave Huntington? Have you talked about this with anyone here?"

"I was waiting for you. I think you know how much I respect your..."

"Then *don't leave*, Buck. You're *not* ready!" I raised my voice, unable to hold back. "You're just considering the Second and Third Steps, trying to come into an understanding of your spirituality, and don't even have a feel for the emotional release that surrender into..."

Buck tried to sound determined, "The pastor tells me *that's* a lot of sentimental bullshit; that what I need is will power to show God and the world that I've changed my ways and that the strength of his church members will support me. I told him I'd start going to church every Sunday."

"And Sarah agrees with this?"

"I think she wants me out of here. She doesn't take any responsibility for my drinking and doesn't like me looking at whether or not our marriage is viable. She thinks if she has me home she can be a better wife and she can make sure I don't drink."

"But your father must think that treatment is important for you. He's talked with Dr. Segen and I thought he was trying to be on the same page as the treatment team."

"He doesn't like the fact that Huntington doesn't use medications. He thinks that with the right anti-anxiety and anti-depressant medications together with sleeping aids I'll be fine. He tells me that Alcoholics Anonymous is for weaklings who need to stay in their sniveling groups, living their lives crying on each others' shoulders."

"He said *that*?" I could feel my muscles tense.

"He said that with a little effort on my part and some good psychotropic meds I'd be feeling better about myself in no time."

"And maintain your sobriety?"

Buck looked as me nervously, searching for the right words to continue. "He said I'd be able to drink again, like a responsible person. He said I just needed to get medially stabilized and approach life more maturely."

I paused a long time, feeling helpless in challenging the forces that were camping in Buck's decision to leave, and providing him a quick and easy return to his system of denial. "I can't agree with you less. I believe what I believe and hold it strongly. If it weren't for Huntington and AA I'd be dead!"

Buck paused a long time, his blue eyes filling and his words shaky, "I know how you feel, John. I know." Buck got up from his chair and moved closer to the window, clasping his hands behind his back; seemingly determined in his decision.

"Your mind is made up?"

Buck watched the doe disappear into the thicket beyond the garden. "I have to try, and think that if I put my mind to it I can live normally again. You know it's not that I haven't learned anything here. I know where drinking can take me, that if I had kept going it would have killed me. Don't you think that might even be enough to keep me going; to keep me drinking like Joe Normal out there?"

I slammed my mug onto the table, "No, I don't!" Again there was a long pause. "Buck, you're a good man. You know I believe in the efforts you're making here at Huntington, and if you need to try it again; to go out there and try to drink responsibly – when you find you can't, I want you to return to us." I tried to calm down.

Buck nervously turned, leaning against the window sill, brushing back a tear and folding his arms across his broad chest, "You really don't think that..."

"I don't, Buck! I'd like to say I do, but I just can't. It goes against everything I believe in about recovery and everything I've learned about you in relation to what you need."

"I have to try." Buck moved toward me, offering me his hand. I shook it, and he again backed away, seeming embarrassed in his decision, returning his gaze out the window.

"But if you come back Buck, I want you to make me a promise." Buck turned toward me, not wanting to ask, as I continued. "That you won't be returning for your wife, your father or your pastor; that if you come back to Huntington you'll be coming back *for Buck*." Little more could be said. I reached in my wallet pulling out my business card and handed it to Buck. "Don't hesitate being in touch with me. OK?"

I returned to the office, closed the door and kicked the desk, "Damn it. Damn this fucking disease!" I allowed Buck to follow through in telling both Dr. Segen, and Gerry about his decision in group. Though others made their concerted efforts, including Jim who threatened to physically block his leaving, by noon Buck had signed against medical advice and was on his way – his triumphant father meeting him in the parking lot and helping him with his luggage.

Before heading into the afternoon group session Jim stopped into the office, looking impulsively about, seeming unsure about his reasons for remaining at Huntington now that Buck thought he could handle it on his own. Our eyes met, and I just knew what he was considering. I could feel my earlier anger again surfacing, "Don't *even think* about going there, Jim!

Jim threw up his arms in surrender, "I know, I know! I just wanted to know what you thought?"

"Now do the next right thing and get your ass into group!" I laughed!

"I'm going, I'm going!"

A somber silence fell over Huntington for the rest of the day and into the next. Jean discharged from treatment on Tuesday, returning to her medical practice and promising to keep close contacts with the house. Peter, with the group's blessing had decided to look for a different occupation - leaving the funeral business, and Jim seemed to be working harder than ever; frightened by Buck's decision and his own impulsivity. Maxine came back to the house on Wednesday and the group focused its efforts on making her feel both welcome and comfortable. She pushed or pulled her small oxygen tank, and though all of us knew when Max was coming down the hall it was now that much more apparent. She was taking a course of medication and vitamins to insure better strength and was scheduled to return to the hospital weekly for her chemotherapy treatments, after which she felt exhausted for about two days before regaining her strength, preparing for the next infusion.

"I'm going to beat this," Maxine stated emphatically, standing in the office, her head shaved to avoid the inevitable embarrassment of hair falling out. She looked more feminine than ever before, sporting a pink head scarf, wearing her jeans and a pretty flowered blouse; plastic oxygen lines leading to her nose – and her coughing into a Kleenex.

I felt her determination, "If anyone is going to beat cancer, you will, Max! I don't know of anyone with more determination than you."

"Cancer? I'm not talking about cancer; hell I've got that under control! I'm talking about my alcoholism!"

I felt the irony and deeply, pausing and holding its' importance. "You really do get it, don't you, Max! Alcoholism truly is as bad as cancer."

"Doesn't take much to fight the cancer, I guess. Just do what the doctors tell you to do, show up for your treatments, but this alcoholism thing is, well..." Maxine searched for her words.

"More insidious," I jumped in.

She looked at me like I was from a foreign land, "So what the hell does that mean?"

I could feel my face redden, "I mean alcoholism is more difficult to define, that it creeps in slowly and silently and one doesn't recognize it until it's in place."

"Maybe, but that's the way cancer got me...but look at Buck, recognizing he's an alcoholic and then...well then he..."

"Vacillates?"

Max laughed and coughed deeply into her tissue, breathing deeply from the oxygen, "Cut with the big words. Just say what the hell you mean, and *yes* I *do* know what that means! We begin to get shaky in our beliefs; thinking we really are OK, until it bite us in the ass again."

"That's denial rearing its ugly head, trying to take us back into the comfort of our illusions about life and what we want to believe rather than grasping the reality of the way things are."

"Sometimes when I'm waking up and before I'm fully into the day, I imagine I'm a young girl again, before the aging, the alcoholism and the cancer. And then I feel the plastic tubes and remember where I am and what I am."

I felt the pain in the reality of her words, "And who would have thought?"

"Who *could* have thought?"

"Max, it never crossed our minds when we were younger wondering about where life would take us, that we would one day find ourselves with cancer or as an alcoholic or drug addict. But those things happen. The important thing is that we recognize them, rally out of our denial, and learn to deal with them."

"And how do we say it? Learning to…" She looked to me to complete the phrase.

"Learning to live life on life's terms."

"I like that. It makes things easier. It's just coming to grips with the reality of the way things are. But where does hope fit in to all of this?"

Max was searching for something to hold onto. "Living life on life's terms doesn't mean that miracles don't surround us constantly. The reality of the way things truly are, isn't always apparent, and the part that isn't apparent lifts us higher, and *when we least expect it.*"

"You mean coincidences?"

I looked deeply into Maxine's imploringly searching eyes, "There are no coincidences, Max, only miracles!"

Friday afternoon came and I was exhausted. Joanne and I went out for an old fashioned Wisconsin fish fry and movie with friends, and fighting an especially heavy snowstorm on the way home were glad to be in the warmth of our family room. Watching the evening news I fell asleep in my recliner as Joanne started watching David Letterman and then drifted off on the couch. I bolted upright to a ringing phone and checking the clock saw that it was near midnight. Joanne jumped up, as parents do, no matter how long it'd been since our son had moved out into his own life, wondering what had happened and reaching the phone before I did. I was right behind her in the hallway. She answered, and after saying "Hold on, John's right here," looked at me curiously, handing me the phone.

"Hello."

"John," there was a long pause, as I recognized the voice, "John, this is Sarah Jaeger." She was sobbing. "It's Buck!" Again there was just Sarah's sobbing and an even longer pause.

"Sarah," my heart sank, "Buck...is Buck all right? Is he there with you?" There was silence and I thought the worst, "Sarah, is Buck *there* with you?"

A faint and shaky voice responded, "Yes John. Buck's here, but not very...very coherent. He's drunker than I've ever seen him. When he comes out of his stupor he won't talk with me; just mutters...says he wants you and then slips into unconsciousness again."

I knew where they lived, about five miles away, and knew it would be pointless talking to Buck on the phone, even if his wife could wake him. "I'm on my way, Sarah. With the snow it'll take me a bit, but I'll be there. Is there any more booze in the house?"

"No, he brought a bottle home...and...and had it down before I got here. God damn it, I thought I could..." she started sobbing uncontrollably, "thought I could, could help him control his..."

"I'm on my way." I hung up the phone, looking at Joanne leaning against the wall, "Damn this disease. I should have been more firm about his leaving Huntington. He's just a kid, listening to his damned father who can't accept his son being an alcoholic. The bastard probably thinks his genes are perfect! I've got to go, Joanne. I'll be back when I can."

Joanne looked at me helplessly, not trying to stop me. She'd been here with me before. She reached for my leather jacket and handed it to me along with my gloves. "Be careful out there, John."

I was fully awake, my adrenaline pumping as I brushed the snow off the old Blazer windows, the door creaking badly, flung open by the wind as I climbed in, engaged the engine and threw the transmission into 4 Wheel Drive. The tires cut through the snow as I headed out into the country to where Buck and Sarah lived. It was a funny thing about what I was doing, and often I found myself questioning about crossing boundary lines with the residents at Huntington. It was a fine line I felt myself walking. If it were any other form of mental health involvement I'd be accused of crossing those boundaries, moving beyond the patient-client relationship, and yet this was somehow different. If I weren't a recovering alcoholic people might have looked at it that way, but I didn't and few others did either. This was what we called Twelfth Step work. It was about *carrying the message of recovery* and especially during those times when one might carry that message most effectively. I questioned how Buck, drunk as I expected to find him could appreciate that tonight, but somehow I knew this would be the moment Buck needed to feel the depths of his utter uncontrollability in the face of his alcoholism – and I was being called to be the messenger. However difficult it was for people to understand, it was the Twelfth Step that continued to keep *me* sober. It's how the program works, and any recovering person who have worked all of the steps understood it.

Pulling into their drive I didn't think about how I would handle the situation, I just reacted, relying on a greater force than my own to direct me. Leaving deep footprints in the snow on the way up the walk, the twinkling lights on the tree in the front window cast a warming glow on the snow covered lawn, giving the illusion and metaphoric denial of the truth now facing Buck again. Knocking on the front door, there was no answer. I entered, finding Buck's black lab nuzzling me further into the hallway. So often I had heard Buck affectionately talk about his dog, wishing she could be brought into Huntington to see him.

"Maizie," I stooped to pet the beautiful animal, "Where's Buck, girl? Where's Buck?" I got up and Maizie nuzzled me further down the hallway. Sarah coming through the kitchen sobbing and not saying a word motioned me to follow her into the back bedroom; the smell of alcohol and vomit hanging in the air. Buck lay crumpled on his side, wearing only boxer shorts and those soaked in his urine, his jeans and sweatshirt covered in pools of vomit and laying on the floor between the bed and bathroom. There are many ways I had heard alcoholics talk about what their *bottoms* looked like, when they had finally reached them. This was the first time I was looking into Buck's, and before he could recognize it as his own. I tried to take charge of the situation, seeing how desperate Sarah was, "How long has he been like this?" I reached for his arm, checking his pulse and respirations. He seemed to be stable enough and even given his young age which could find him more quickly affected with alcohol poisoning, his history of usage found him with quite a high tolerance. I wasn't too concerned regarding his present level of safety, although one could never be certain.

"I got home at about 9 o'clock and found him lying on the bed, and with that empty vodka bottle next to him." She pointed to the empty bottle of Absolut. "About 11 he got up, and trying to get to the bathroom didn't make it and started throwing up all over his clothes and the floor. I tried helping him get cleaned up, but he just stripped off his clothes and fell into the bed, mumbling to himself and calling out your name. He's been out for a few of hours."

I moved closer to the bed, my feelings of compassion outweighing the stench, looking beyond the raging disease and onto a decent human being who I knew was again locked within its ugly grasp. I put my hand on his shoulder, shaking him gently. "Buck!" There was a simple muttering. "Buck, Buddy? Are you with us?" There was little movement, and I tried again, shaking him more forcefully. Finally he rolled onto his back, his great chest heaving deeply as he coughed his way to consciousness; the stench of his breath overpowering, his blue eyes opening and trying to focus on me.

"John? Tha..tha...that...?"

"Yup, it's me." I waited, watching him blinking and trying to focus. Buck started gagging. I grabbed his arm, pulling him to a sitting position, the smell of urine and vomit finding me forcing back my own wanting to gag.

"It's kicked...kicked my a...a...ass... pretty bad!"

"I know." I tried to talk slowly, making certain he understood what I was saying. "How about I see if I can get you into the Detox Unit tonight?" Buck lifted his head, trying to focus more intently, his eyes filling with tears.

"Oh f...fuck....jus...jus..."

"Buck, you could be dangerously..."

He understood, dropping his head back onto the bed in resignation, "F...fuck...just get me there."

I helped him shower, steadying him under the shower head, and helped him get dressed. On the way out the door Buck nearly fell over Maizie, nudging him with her wet nose, knowing something was amiss. Sarah tried saying something, but Buck wasn't listening, his shoulders sunken under his coat as I helped him out to the Blazer.

The drive back to the treatment center was subdued and quiet; my not thinking Buck would understand much of what I had to offer, and Buck sobering just enough to feel terrible. In one sense I wanted to be as supportive as I could, and yet allow him any moment of half-clarity to feel the depth of the despair I knew he needed to feel. Finally, nearly spinning out on the slick road as I turned up the hospital's long wooded drive, I broke the silence, *"This has to be bottom, Buck!* It can't get much worse than this." We both knew we were looking at the same thing, *the utter uncontrollability* of active alcoholism.

"I know. I f...f...fucking know! I fuck, fuck, fucking god damn know!"

I felt it, deep in my guts. Reflecting back, remembering my own beginnings; I had been there, and knew deep down, that but for the Grace of God I could *still* be there, or dead. It wasn't that many years before that I had been on the same Detox Unit. I remembered the utter feeling of helplessness and hopelessness. Although Buck was starting from scratch, it was another hope-filled beginning for him. Before I left him sitting on the hospital bed with a nurse taking his vitals, he reached out his shaky hand, "Hope...I hope you're there, John...there again...to...to meet me at Huntington."

"You've got to do it for yourself this time!"

"I know. I f...f...fucking know! I...I just hope you're there to..."

I took his hand, grasping it firmly, "I hope I am too!"

V

Daybreak

Traditionally Christmas week was the beginning of a quiet time at Huntington – sometimes *too* quiet! The residents who were further in their treatment were given passes and spent the holiday away from the center with family or friends. Although the policy for Christmas, it was quite the opposite for New Year's Eve and Day – that time of year when *celebration* and *alcohol* were words used synonymously by a general public. Few, if any passes were given, and at Huntington we tried to celebrate the day with a barbecue; no matter how cold it was out on the deck – a couple of brave guys would weather the temperature and grill steaks and chicken, and there would be the board games. Trivial Pursuit continued as a regular recovery game at the center, and the residents were learning they could enjoy themselves immensely without alcohol or drug use; something they had forgotten such a long time ago.

I didn't visit Buck on the Detox Unit. I almost did, and then thought better not to. It was important for him to feel the depth and loneliness of his relapse and the deeper bottom he had fallen into. I had talked with staff on the unit who let me know that Buck had refused to see anyone from the outside, even Sarah when she dropped off a suitcase of the things he would need. He refused calls from both his father and Pastor Burnum, and somehow I took that as a good sign of Buck thinking for himself once again.

Today was Christmas Eve in the early afternoon, and at Maxine's ordering Jim and a couple of new guys to treatment, somewhat reluctant to accommodate her barking orders, agreed to locate an artificial tree they were told was packed away in a third floor closet. Jim had become very protective of Maxine, almost like a grandson would his favorite grandmother. There was something wonderfully warm about their relationship, although to someone just hearing them for the first time they sounded like a cat and dog challenging each other; one filling a certain need in the other. It all spoke very deeply about how far Jim had come in his treatment and the new insights about life he was finding within himself. One couldn't say he was less impulsive however, and that aspect of his personality mixed with Maxine's barking orders afforded a gentle and yet distinctive character to the house over the holidays – like something you'd expect to find in a Charles Dickens novel.

"Three strong guys and you can't get a fake tree out of a closet? You've *got* to be kidding!" Maxine hacked and coughed at the top of her voice, standing in the stairwell and wearing a denim scarf, her oxygen tank in hand following behind her.

Jim stuck his head over the third floor banister, "We'll have it and the boxes of ornaments down there in a minute. Bet if these old treatment center ornaments could talk they'd tell us…"

"Just get it all down here; we don't need anymore stories about ghosts from Huntington's past."

Leaning further over the ledge, Jim's eyes widened, "What ghosts?"

"Where have you been? I thought everyone here has heard about the ghost in room number 5! Come on, come on, get the damn tree *down* here!"

"Max, *what* ghost in room number 5? That's *my* room!"

Max coughed a laugh, "If I'd remembered that was your room I wouldn't have told you – a long story that Carrie from the night shift told me, involving a guy who was in that room *last* Christmas. I'll explain later, but for now will you get that godforsaken tree down these steps?" She coughed deeply, repositioning her oxygen behind her. "I'm trying to live long enough to decorate it!"

I was in the office listening to the banter and thinking that if anyone could survive on pure strength of will and determination, Maxine could. And then I reminded myself again as she had reminded me earlier, that recovery from alcoholism was entirely different - that though it takes a good measure of determination, it takes an even greater measure of surrendering to *A Higher Power* for the strength *beyond us* that we need to both maintain and enrich our recoveries. While listening to Maxine barking her orders as the two new guys dragged the boxed tree down the hall and into the TV lounge - Jim balancing boxes of ornaments in his arms, stuck his head into the office, looking perplexed and even a bit anxious.

"You guys are holding out on me! *What's the story about the ghost in room # 5?*" A box of ornaments came crashing to the floor, and from the sound of things, smashed half its' contents.

I laughed, and stooped to retrieve the sorry box of trimmings, "Jim, a big guy like you, fighting for your life and caring about some story about a..."

"Hey..." Jim's attention turned toward the front door, opening slowly.
"Talk about Ghosts of Christmas! Welcome back, Buck!" Jim put the remaining boxes on the floor and moved toward him, shaking his hand enthusiastically. "Glad you're back."

I moved out of the office and into the hallway, Buck eyeing me cautiously over Jim's shoulder, his eyes welling with tears. "It's...it's been a coup...couple of ugly days." Buck was unsteady; more out of nervousness and embarrassment, his eyes not leaving mine.

"Welcome back, Buck! I walked toward him, shook his hand and then hugged him. "Glad you're here."

Again our eyes met, "I wanted to believe you'd be back here; guess I knew you'd be back if things didn't work your way."

Jim grabbed Buck's suitcase, and additional bags of things Sarah had packed when she learned Buck had decided to return to treatment. "Where are we putting him, John?"

"Same room; haven't given it up to anyone new."

"You knew I'd be coming back, didn't you John?" Buck nodded his head and shrugged his shoulders, as if to say, 'You told me so.'

"Buck, I wouldn't wish what you went through on anyone. Not only the physical stuff, but the emotional collapse."

Buck stopped in his tracks, gritted his teeth and set his gaze on the floor, "You *do* know what it's like."

I motioned Buck toward the office. Jim, seeing that this was getting personal, slapped Buck on the back and edged his way past us and down the hall, carrying Buck's luggage to his room. Maybe Jim *was* becoming just a bit less impulsive. Buck eased himself into the office chair.

I began slowly, "We've talked before; you know I've been there too." Things grew silent, with my waiting for Buck to take the lead, watching him returning his gaze to the floor and growing more nervous. I continued to wait.

"John, I ah...I want to thank you...for..." Buck lifted his head and looked into my eyes; his face grimacing, tears flowing freely down his cheeks, "for doing what you did for me the other night. I don't know of anyone who would have – could have done that for me....ah..." Buck shook his head, "ah...not *anyone!*"

"I believe in you, Buck!" I could feel my own eyes well up with emotion.

"I know. You *proved* that, and *again* when I no longer could believe in myself. I really thought I could control my drinking, that I could drink responsibly; but somewhere..." Buck paused, his eyes focusing on the window, as if taking himself back to that awful night. "Somewhere between the second and third drink I knew I couldn't stop. It was over; I couldn't control it. Everything I hoped I could do; thought I had regained and wanted to believe about myself was gone.

It was fucking gone. If I had had…" Buck nodded his head, affirming to himself what he was about to say, "…if I had had another bottle of vodka I would have kept going. In such a short time I found myself wanting to end it; wanting it over – I wanted *to die*." Buck again faced me, and paused, collecting his words, "And there you were, like some proverbial angel…pulling me back from the gates of my own hell; vomit, piss and all – there *you* were, John." Again there was silence, Buck slowly got to his feet, moved to the windows searching the landscape, and finally turned back toward me, "Why?"

I shrugged my shoulders, "Because I believe in you."

"Coming out late at night in the middle of a snow storm, having to smell my vomit and piss, standing an almost unconscious drunken slug up under a shower…?"

I cut in, as I took my turn staring out the window at the sun-drenched and cold snow-covered landscape, "*And* because I believe in the process. I have to, for my own recovery to continue. Don't you see it Buck? My belief in you is my belief in myself. Would I do it for everyone? Maybe I wouldn't - not if I thought someone hadn't reached enough of his bottom to be workable; before he could see the entire darkness of his uncontrollability."

"I'm not sure I understand how you can…?"

"In a way it's selfishness, I guess. Through you I can see how bad it could again be for me. It's different for those of us who've been in recovery for awhile and who've worked all Twelve Steps. We need to focus on other people *early* in their journeys. It's not that we don't continue to work The Steps – we do. But in working my Twelfth Step, through my carrying the message to others and helping them work their program, I insure my continuing focus on my own recovery, through helping them focus on theirs."

"*Selfish?* It's the most selfless thing a friend could do for a friend."

"Its how recovery works - how The Twelve Steps work." We continued our gaze out the windows and onto the blanketed gardens, catching sight of the white-tailed doe entering the clearing this side of the wooded thicket. I pointed, "Looks like your friend's back."

Buck caught sight of the animal, the sun glistening off the doe's brown back, her sniffing the air and looking straight at us. "She was here the day I left."

"She's welcoming you back, Buck."

"I love animals and wildlife."

"I know. I met your black lab friend, Maizie."

Buck beamed, "She's a beautiful dog, isn't she? She could win any Frisbee contest! Her love for me is so unconditional. I could be the sorriest loser around, and she'd be there for me."

"She let me in the other night, and nuzzled me down the hall to where I found you."

Buck sighed, "Wish I could have her here."

"And Sarah?"

"Not now, John. I don't even want to talk with her. She can leave messages if she wants, but I need some time to think."

"And the others?"   "It'll be a long time before I want to talk with my father again, and you know, it's not because I'm embarrassed; I'm fucking pissed! It can't be *his way* ever again."

"Pissed at him?"

Buck thought for a long moment, "I guess I'm pissed at myself for not believing enough in myself to stand for what I was beginning to hold onto, letting myself fall under his wanting me to be perfect and not an alcoholic son." Buck's face reddened. "Well fuck him! And that bastard Burnum - it'll be a god-damned long time before I set foot in his church again."

"So, this time it's different?"

Again Buck looked intently into me, "Like you said John, this time it's for Buck Jaeger. It can't be for anybody else. I'm ready to start over. I'm ready to begin work on The First Step."

"The First Step, what are you talking about? You haven't learned that you have absolutely no control over alcohol, that with it your life remains totally unmanageable? You haven't learned *even that?*"

"Are you kidding?" Buck looked at me as though I had lost my senses, "If there's anything that I've learned over the past week it's that I will never *ever* again have control over the stuff. It's beaten me, and will again if I let it."

"Then you're not starting over, Buck. It just took you *one more time out there* to learn that you don't have control. I'd say you've graduated, more experienced than most from The First Step. Time to move into The Second Step, *We came to believe that a power greater than ourselves could restore us to sanity.*"

Buck's chest and shoulders sagged, "I just told you I'm never stepping foot inside a church again. If I need to…"

"Who's talking about church? We're talking about *coming to believe.* The Second Step doesn't say anything about how we do that?"

Buck relaxed and brightened, "OK, where do I begin?"

"You go and get unpacked and settled. I'm going to put together a packet of readings and materials to get you going, and a couple of books you might consider getting from the bookstore in the village." I put out my hand. "Do we have a deal?"

Buck took it, "We've got a deal."

"Welcome back to Huntington!"

"I *knew* you'd be here." Buck headed toward the hall and in the doorway turned, "I'm going to make us both proud of our recoveries, John."

"I know you will. I knew you would *that first time* you came into this office."

Again I could see the emotion welling up in Buck, could feel it filling me. Our eyes met as Buck paused, trying to find more words. There was nothing else to be said; he said it all in a humble nod, turned and headed down the hall.

I continued staring into the empty doorway, whispering "Go to it, Buck! You can do it Buddy!"

I gave shift turnover to Dale and Rebecca who didn't mind working Christmas Eve, so long as they had Christmas morning with their families. I didn't mind working the morning, so long as I was off on Christmas Eve. Rick our son would be home by the time I got there. His holiday break from the university was short this year, with his just being able to spend a few days with us. He was working on his Masters Degree now, and things weren't as easy as when he was an undergrad. Recovery taught me that the quality of our time together was so much more important than the amount of time spent. Since Rick was an infant we always celebrated Christmas Eve, finding some way to sneak Santa's gifts into the house. Those times were past and we came to enjoy quieter Christmases. My sobriety had afforded the comfort of simplicity. We were looking forward to lighting a fire in the fireplace, exchanging a few gifts and going through the photo albums, and perhaps watching a video of a Christmas past. My former obsessive perfectionism would again be pointed out, and I would find myself sighing – grateful to appreciate gifts that weren't wrapped in color-coordinated trim; grateful for the peace of mind and the warmth of family. It would be an early night for me, having to get up for work in the morning.

A gentle snow fell in the early morning hours, and as Joanne and Rick slept in, I got ready and quietly slipped out of the house. The smell of hearth embers continuing to glow through the night, mixed with the cold flakes of snow and the neighboring church bells tolling 6AM afforded a gentle feeling rising in my spirit. I was happy to be alive and to be at peace with myself. I seemed to be the only person out on the country road leading to Huntington, cutting the first tracks in the snow, playing excerpts from *Handel's Messiah* on my Blazer stereo, wondering what the day would bring, and watching as the clouds began to clear into an open sky.

I grabbed hold of the straw broom at the base of the Huntington steps, sweeping them clear as I climbed to the door covered in a huge pine wreath and cascading bow. Almost snowed-over footprints followed up the steps and again retreated, and near the door was a shopping bag in which was placed a small gift wrapped in green foil and red satin ribbon. I dusted the snow off of the parcel and carried it into the house. Carrie from the night shift positioned herself in the office doorway as I stamped the snow off my shoes on the mat just inside the door.

"Merry Christmas John."

"Merry Christmas Carrie. Look what someone left at the front door? It must have been out there most of the night. Maybe Santa was trying to get it to you!" Carrie stepped aside as I entered the office, handing her the bag while I hung up my coat.

"Hmmm, guess we're both out of luck," Carried fumbled with the card enclosure. "It's for Buck."

"Why wouldn't whoever brought it knock, even if it was after hours and the door was locked?"

If I had thought a bit further I might have guessed, but preoccupied with getting ready for my shift, asked "How is everybody? Did everyone have a good Christmas Eve?"

"Wish that were the case, John. Max was taken to the hospital in the village. During the PM shift the group was gathered around the Christmas tree, trying to make the best of the holiday here at the house. There were a lot of stories and remembrances and some festive foods that the hospital had catered in for the residents. There were a few laughs and Maxine getting caught up in the moment started coughing more than usual and seemed to have a more difficult time catching her breath. She started having chest pains and to be on the safe side an ambulance took her to the hospital in the village."

"Oh, not at Christmas," my heart sank. "Is there any word?"

"The last we heard it was determined she had had a heart attack, and there *was* extensive damage. She's been made as comfortable as is possible in the ICU. Her family is there with her."

My soul ached and all I could feel was emptiness in the pit of my stomach. "Does everyone in the house know?"

"Not yet - they understand she had the shortness of breath and had to be taken to the hospital. Everyone believes she just over-exerted herself, given her chemo treatments, and they're expecting she'll be returning to celebrate Christmas with us today. I expect that Jim might be up earlier than usual. He kept asking if we had any more information about Max before he went to bed. I'm glad you're here to explain it to him. You know him so much better than I do."

"Jim is going to have a hard time, but everyone in the house has come to feel close to Maxine. She's been the glue that's held everyone together at times, and now since her cancer - they've been doing a great job of supporting and holding her together."

"Hopefully we'll have better news this morning!" Carrie looked at me, thinking that if she could convince me she might be able to convince herself.

"We can only hope. By the way, what's the stuff you've been telling Maxine about the ghost in Room #5?"

Carrie looked at me, her face broadening into a grin. "I didn't have anything to do with it, John. Max concocted it, dragged me into it to add support to the preposterous story for when she told Jim. I played along and he fell for it – hook, line and sinker! She was having more fun with it over the past couple days, reporting every new nervous muscle twitch he'd display, as he begged to hear more about the mysterious apparition. She had everyone in the house *in on* her adventure. It's been great fun. I'm surprised nobody slipped it to you yesterday."

"You're as bad as she is." I laughed.

"John, you would have done the same. It's been so much fun watching Jim react. He's so animated and free-spirited in his early recovery."

"Anything else I need to know before…"

"Other than Maxine going to the hospital, it's been a quiet night. Peter called, saying he was having some difficult times on his pass home, talking about difficulties with his wife and alcohol cravings he didn't anticipate, and that he was going to return early this afternoon if not before. I'm guessing it will be quiet for awhile until everyone gets up. You know you don't have Morning Meditation until 10 AM, given that this is Christmas."

I looked at the mysterious gift Carrie was still holding. "Going to keep that package?"

Carrie handed it to me. "You know that Buck is going to have to open it here in the office, especially given that you found it outside on the steps. No telling who might have…"

I thought for a moment, "Bet it's from his wife, Sarah."

"Well, why didn't she call or at least knock at the…"

"Buck doesn't want to see her." I thought to myself and muttered to Carrie, "This might be a more difficult Christmas than we expected."

"Want me to stay on for awhile longer, John?"

"No, it's time you get home to your family. You should get a couple hours sleep and then celebrate your Christmas."

"I'm in luck. David's cooking – started last night. He's not bad in the kitchen when he puts his mind to it." Carrie reached behind the door for her coat. "Hope you have a good day, and again, Merry Christmas. If things get difficult give me a call."

"We'll get through this, Carrie. I just hope Maxine makes it. "Merry Christmas to your family." I watched as she headed down the hall and out the door. I poured a cup of coffee from the pot and took my seat behind the desk, my eyes on Buck's green and red decorated gift in front of me. Turning my attention toward the windows, it was near 7:30 and the sun was just beginning to rise across the lawns and flower beds. Sipping my coffee, I noticed another movement at the window, a reflection from behind me, and realized I wasn't alone.

"John..."

I swiveled in the office chair, my eyes meeting Jim's, almost staring through me, as if deep in thought, and yet..."

"John, I just got a call on my cell phone." Jim's hair was disheveled, and he wasn't wearing more than a T-shirt and sweatpants – and was barefooted, obviously having just gotten up.

"Good morning, Jim. Merry Christmas; want some coffee? Carrie makes quite the eye-opener." I didn't wait for him to respond, getting up and pouring a cup of the brew for him.

"I got a call, John. It was Max."

"But she's..." I didn't know what to think. Carrie had told me she was in ICU, and I didn't think she could be making a call.

"A nurse called and then put Max on the phone. I could hardly understand her – she sounded so weak."

Again, I didn't know how to respond, still not believing her call was possible. I questioned further, "She called to wish you a Merry Christmas?"

"She didn't mention Christmas, almost as if she didn't have enough energy."

I didn't respond, giving Jim enough time to collect his thoughts.

"Her words came slowly and were so determined, weak and raspy. All she said to me was 'Jim, promise me...promise me you'll hold on...hold on to your recovery...hold on as if it were the most important thing in your life.' She sighed, rested a moment, and then continued, 'Jim, promise me.'

I didn't know what to say. I started asking her when she thought she'd be back here at Huntington, and it was almost like she didn't hear me. Again, she said, coughing and even weaker, 'Don't let this disease get you, Jim. Promise me, Jim...' Her words cut right into my heart." Jim thumped his chest with his open palm. "Again she said, 'Promise me, Jim...' I felt her words so deeply my chest hurt, and I felt myself stumbling on my words."

I felt Jim's pain, "Maxine cares a great deal about you."

Jim paused, collecting his words, "I said...I said Max, *I promise*." Jim could hardly get the words out, brushing the tears back with his arm.

"She loves you like the son she never had."

"All she said was 'Good.' There was a long pause, and the nurse came back on, telling me that Maxine needed to rest, and said goodbye."

I took a sip of my coffee, and Jim taking the cue put his mug to his lips just as the phone rang, startling him – him spilling coffee all over his worn shirt. "Huntington House, John speaking." The doctor on the other end identified himself, slowly giving me the sad information he found himself needing to report. There was a long silence. I didn't, couldn't say any more than "I'm so...so very sorry. I can't believe...believe that..." I listened to his final words and thanked him for calling, looking into Jim's solemn eyes as I hung up the phone. He knew. I slowly reached out for his hand, holding it with both my hands, my heart aching as the reality of the moment took us both.

Tears were flowing freely down Jim's cheeks and he began to sob bitterly. Moments turned into minutes. I continued to hold his hand. "I promised her, John. It was the last thing that was important to her - my recovery."

"She loved you." Again moments turned into longer minutes.

"I want...want to be the one telling the group. I owe it to Max. I want to tell the group at Morning Meditation."

I nodded, understanding. "It's all yours to lead. I'll be there to support you."

"Thanks." Jim looked nervously to the open doorway. "Think I'll just go to my room and think things over."

"OK, Buddy. You need anything, I'll be here." Jim slowly got to his feet, leaving the office. I made a few necessary calls, but promised myself I would allow Jim to announce Max's death to the group at our first morning gathering. Somehow I knew he'd be much more effective than I could be, the group knowing how much Maxine and Jim cared for each other. The morning ticked away; its silence and the fact that it was Christmas seemed somehow surreal, and as I told myself that Max's death would take some time to sink in, Buck walked into the office.

"Who would have ever thought I'd be spending Christmas Day here at Huntington?"

"Feeling a little sorry for yourself?" I reflected as compassionately as I could.

"Not really. I thought about the possibilities as I was shaving, and know I couldn't be at home today." Wearing a simple bright red cotton sweater and new pair of jeans and moccasins, Buck leaned up against the counter, attempting a smile.

I pointed toward the desk, "A gift for you, Buck"

Buck snickered, "You shouldn't have."

"I didn't! It was sitting in a bag in the snow on the front door steps when I got here this morning."

Buck backed away from it. "It's from Sarah; I can tell by the way its wrapped...guess I'd rather not..."

"It's Christmas, Buck."

"It's Sarah trying to control me again."

I looked at the gift, "Why not open it?"

"Why not leave well enough alone?"

"Buck, think about it." I tried not to sound too patronizing. "I know you're hurt and want to place part of the blame for your relapse outside of yourself, and *yes* I agree that you're family needs to learn a great deal about alcoholism, but give Sarah an opportunity *to begin* to understand."

Buck reached for the gift, shaking it, its contents thudding from off the insides.

I shrugged my shoulders, "Doesn't sound like handcuffs!"

"We'll see." He unwrapped the package and lifted the lid. Inside was a daily meditation book for men, and a bronze recovery pocket token, inscribed with the Serenity Prayer:

> ***God grant me the serenity***
> ***to accept the things I cannot change,***
> ***the courage to change the things I can,***
> ***and the wisdom to know the difference.***

A simple enclosure card read, 'Merry Christmas Buck. This time I promise I won't get in the way. Maizie and I are missing you. I love you, Sarah.'
Buck looked up and into me, not sure what to think.

I saw the opportunity, "Doesn't look like handcuffs!"

"It's great, but I'm not sure I'm ready to see her. It's just too close to *that* night." Buck put the book and token carefully, affectionately back in the box. "I'd better get ready for Morning Meditation. Want me to lead it this morning? Guess I could use my new book!"

"Jim's already asked," I said slowly, looking away. Buck, not understanding my discomfort, wrinkled his brow, but didn't pursue it.

"Any news about Max?"

Again I was uncomfortably looking for the right words. "Let me see if we can get some information to give you all when we gather. I think that since the group is so small we'll meet in the lounge, around the Christmas tree rather than downstairs. How's that sound?"

"See you there, John." Buck got to his feet, holding onto his gift and headed toward the door.

"Think you *might* be talking with Sarah today?"

Buck turned, looking helpless. "I wish I...wish I could, John. I just don't think I can."

"Well, the day is still young!"

"Don't know, John...just don't think I can - anyway, Merry Christmas." Buck left the office, heading down the hall. I checked the clock. It was near 10 AM. I could hear the residents rustling in the kitchen, the cupboard doors banging, cleaning up after their breakfasts. Grabbing our usual meditation book to give to Jim, I closed the door and headed toward the lounge; the soft sounds of instrumental Christmas Carols playing in the background. Looking at the tree, I quickly thought back to yesterday when Jim and Maxine toyed with each other, thriving on each others regard.

The group gathered; a new guy who was admitted to treatment two days before, the two guys who had helped Jim with the tree, a middle-aged female nurse who had been in treatment for about a week, and a young male anesthesiologist. The nurse and anesthesiologist were both facing licensing issues because of being under the influence of drugs and the anesthesiologist was accused of directly diverting drugs from the hospital supplies for his own use. Peter hadn't returned as yet, and maybe that was a sign that things were going better at home; that he had been able to successfully handle his cravings. Jim and Buck were the last to enter the room. It was obvious that Jim had not told him about Maxine. We sat in our circle near the tree, as a piano version of "O Holy Night" played softly in the background.

"Merry Christmas everyone," I began, and we all exchanged our pleasantries, except for Jim who seemed so very preoccupied. I felt his loss – all of our loss, as I handed the meditation book to him, "Jim has asked that he be able to lead this morning's meditation."

Jim slowly took the book, opened it and found the page for December 25th. Shakily he began to read:

"Christmas is a homecoming of the heart, and especially for those of us finding ourselves in recovery from the dependencies we are faced with in our lives. Daybreak arrives with the promise of a new gift – the gift of Our Higher Power being born again and again in our lives, with the deepening understanding of our need to surrender into the miracle of That Power.

How difficult we tend to make such a simple "turning over" of our wills to find the wealth of strength we need in That Power that transcends us. We complicate it by thinking of it as a "giving up" of the will, rather than as an "opening" of the will – an opening to the miraculous forces that transcend our limited comprehension and understanding of existence, our place and purpose in this universe, our reasons for being, living through, and transcending our lives – transcending the forces of our addictions.

Consider the infant; the new life of any infant, and consider the new spirituality born out of our need to locate the strength we no longer have. Christmas is an opportunity to consider the gift of spiritual understanding. Wherever our search leads us, through faiths and belief systems, our spiritual understanding of Our Higher Power becomes our daybreak into new life. And once the gift is given, and the Second Step of our Recovery is finally held, it's a short step into making the Third Step decision to turn our will and lives over to Our Higher Powers' care — through whom we find our strength.

The daybreak of our surrender is a homecoming of the heart and of the soul, and in its new light we find all the strength we could ever need."

Jim was trembling as he closed the book and let it fall into his lap. Everyone felt his tension, showing their concern; their brows wrinkled and leaning closer into the circle — even the newer residents. Jim started his comments, and though he never directly reflected on the reading, what he had to say added an even deeper dimension to it. "Merry Christmas everyone, I…I'm Jim and I'm an alcoholic." The residents murmured their greeting, more concerned about his tears that were beginning to flow.

Buck leaned into him, "You OK, Jim?" I waited, somehow knowing that Jim could handle this.

Jim paused, took a deep breath, and looked about the group, "I had asked John if I could lead the meditation this morning, because I have something to share with all of us. Early this morning, Maxine called me. She was very weak, and still somehow convinced a nurse to make the call and hand her the phone." He smiled, "You know how pushy Maxine can be! Her *'You've got to be kidding'* wouldn't keep a nurse from not allowing her a phone call for long. She called for only one thing. She begged and made me promise that I would do everything I needed to do to nourish…to maintain my recovery. I promised her – *gave her my word.* She got weak, and the nurse took the phone and said goodbye. I came down to John in the office and after I told him what had happened, the office phone rang. It was Maxine's doctor. She was gone."

Jim's tears began to flow freely, as he tried to fight them back on the sleeve of his green sweatshirt, allowing himself to feel the pain again. Buck looked at me as did the others, and then back to Jim. A heavy sadness descended on the group. The only sound was Jim's shallow and short sobbing breaths. Everyone waited for him to continue.

"I…I went back…went back into my room and closed the door, laying on my bed and staring out the window as daybreak's light continued to fill the room. A great calm came over me, and suddenly I felt another. I felt *a presence* in the room. The presence was warm and loving, and somehow I knew…" Jim wiped his eyes, and took a deep breath, "I knew I'd be OK." Jim looked at the others…slapping his chest with his open palm, "I knew…was filled with *the knowledge* I'd be OK."

Jim paused; there wasn't a dry eye in the room – Buck was biting the side of his cheek, tears welling in his eyes. "Jim, that's…"

"There's more." He took another deep breath, "I sat up on my bed and closed my eyes…and I whispered to the forces that be, 'I don't have…don't have a great understanding of God or the forces beyond me; don't have a great understanding of too much, I guess. But I do believe in a power…a power greater than me - a power that guides existence and my life if I'd let it." Jim looked about the group again, "I slowly…so slowly began to pray – like never before, 'I can't control my alcoholism, can't even control my impulsiveness. I believe *You, My Higher Power* can. I surrender all that I am to you – surrender myself into your care."

I couldn't hold back, "Jim, that's so beautifully stated. I know how difficult it is to get to that point. And you've taken us all right there – into the force of that power."

"It's not that I won't have remarkably difficult times. I know. I know how ugly it can get. I've seen it in action…"

Jim looked at Buck and winked. "…but I do know I'll be OK. I have two things to hold onto, the strength of My Higher Power, and the promise I made to Max." He paused again and shrugged his shoulders, "There really is a spirit in room #5, and I'm not leaving her there. When I discharge from Huntington she's coming with me."

The morning meditation continued, with each of the group taking turns reflecting on Maxine, Jim's profound and heartfelt comments, and the reading. Getting to our feet, we gathered in the usual circle, held hands and recited the Serenity Prayer. The hugs that followed were tighter and longer than usual. While Buck was giving me his hug, I heard the front door down the hall fly open, and a frustrated voice trying to control what sounded like large animal.

"Hey, get back here…you can't just…get…get back here…" came the frustrated female voice at the end of the hall. Too late; within a few seconds the sound of thundering pounding paws on the wooden floors reached the French doors of the lounge, and with a bang of her nose pushed them open, bolting into the room. The sleek black lab pushed into the group, found Buck and jumped up on him with such force he was thrown back onto the leather couch with her leaping on top of him.

"Maizie! Oh, Maizie…it's so good to see you girl." He wrestled with her on the couch, holding her on top of him, with her slobbering and licking his face. Everyone, even Jim laughed at the raucous scene unfolding before them.

Sarah stood at the doors, nervous and trying to smile. Buck managed to get out from under Maizie and sat up, as the beautiful animal jumped to the floor, sitting beside Buck and barking her excitement. Buck's eyes caught Sarah's, feeling her discomfort, "Hello Sarah," Buck said slowly and softly, getting to his feet.

The group, feeling the awkwardness said hello to Sarah and excused themselves. I was the last one out, wishing Sarah a Merry Christmas and turning to Buck, "Why not spend some time together?" Buck nodded and Sarah moved toward him and Maizie. I backed out of the room, closing the French doors, smiling to myself again about the miracles that open around us, if we allow them.

It was a Christmas Day I'll long remember. Peter did return to the safety of Huntington – his difficulties with the celebration at home had triggered too many cravings. Buck, who had spent a long time with Sarah and Maizie asked if I though it might be all right if he and Sarah went out for a late Christmas brunch in the village. It didn't take me long to agree, adding only "Just go slow, Buck."

"I will John. You bet I will. I don't want to get into anything heavier today anyway. We'll save that for the family therapist."

"So you've decided to see Deb? She's already asked if you and Sarah had decided to enter into therapy with her."

"We did a lot of talking through the morning. There are a lot of things we'll need to be working on. Trust me, *a lot!*"

Jim walked into the office, looking as though he had just gotten up from a nap. Buck was right on him.

"You doing OK? You had some amazing things to say. Thanks to you and some of the things John gave me to read, I think I'm beginning to understand what the Second and Third Steps mean. This morning you had a way of just putting it all out there – straight from your guts."

"Thanks. I just let it happen, I guess...just let what was flowing flow."

"Third Step...it's all about making a decision, isn't it?"

"Sounds so simple, and yet it's so fucking hard. Making a decision and then *getting the hell out of my way!* It sounds so easy, but it's not. Max put it this way, just last week, 'Grace is and Grace comes.' All we have to do is make the decision to turn our will and lives over to Our Higher Power, and remain open to the wealth of grace that is always afforded us. We just have to let the miracle begin to happen."

"Max told you that last week?"

"Ya, but it took until this morning before I got it! And I'm telling you guys, it took everything out of me."

"You look a little wiped out!"

"It exhausted me, just got up from a nap! It's been such an emotionally rocky morning. I still can't believe Max is gone, and yet she'll remain with me – the driving force in my recovery I guess, like some patron saint!"

"How about you joining Sarah and me for something to eat in the village?"

"You should be spending that time alone with her."

"Hmmm, might be better if you were with us. I want to keep it light today. We'll save the heavier stuff for Deb's office...my treat."

"I didn't have leaving the treatment center today approved by Gerry. I hadn't planned on leaving the house. But I've got the time; won't be getting visitors until this evening." Jim looked over to me for my approving his leaving the grounds without Gerry's OK, as I had Buck's earlier.

"Why not, seems I'm breaking all the house rules today, anyway!"

Buck's face broadened into a mischievous smile as he crossed his arms on his red-sweatered chest, "Ah...John, how about breaking one more...just one more *tiny* rule?"

"You guys are going to get me fired!" I paused, "Well...it's Christmas, maybe the firing squad will take that into consideration. *What rule* am I breaking now?"

"Just a tiny one," he snickered. Buck whistled, and from down the hall came the furious thudding cadence of heavy paws slipping on the wooden floor. Maizie slid into the office and heeled next to Buck, nuzzling him with her cold nose and looking up at him in anticipation. Buck led her over to my chair, patted her affectionately, told her to sit and when she settled, told her to stay.

"I *will* get fired for this!" Maizie searched my questioning face, nuzzled my hand with her wet nose, and I began petting her and scratching behind the ears.

"Well...well maybe I can...can do it just this one time!" Laughter filled the office; all three of us, and with it, Maizie took to barking.

"Who's in charge here anyway?" Again Maizie nuzzled my hand, putting her head on my lap.

Jim jabbed Buck in the ribs, "John, I thought recovery was about *giving up* control?"

I continued my focus on the beautiful animal, "OK Maizie, you're in charge – just this once." Turning my attention to the two guys in front of me, "Will you get your butts out of here? Maizie and I have to talk about Buck's *aftercare,* for when he gets home." Maizie looked up at me, cocking her head; her big dark eyes attempting to understand, as I continued to pet her, "Don't we girl?"

VI

Controlled by the Will –
Released by the Heart

If addiction and it's fortress of denial wreck havoc on ones relationship with oneself, relationships with others are left shattered in the rubble of its storm. There are those times in life when couples intent on saving their marriages, family or personal relationships are unable to sort through the issues on their own - no matter how dedicated and hard working they are, it's difficult seeing the proverbial "forest for the trees." Often, and with most residents in close personal relationships, we encourage sessions with Deb, our family therapist. Buck and Sarah had taken that step, and yet there was a certain reluctance on both their parts, almost as if they didn't want to lay open the specifics of their marriage – Buck feeling controlled by his wife, and Sarah wanting to save the marriage but not seeing her part in their difficulties - much less in Buck's addictive behaviors. Philosophically the treatment team tried to help marriages become healthier and more viable. Sometimes that wasn't possible, and it was better for both parties to go their separate ways. If it needed to happen for a recovering alcoholic or addict, what better place for that to occur than when in treatment – being supported by ones peers and therapists.

Maxine's funeral found us all reflecting on her strength. The residents went as a group in the Huntington van, as the service was held in the evening. I had gone home after my shift, meeting the group for the visitation and service where Buck and I found ourselves keeping close eyes on Jim, allowing him a few quiet moments at the open casket. I watched as he pulled a bronze recovery token inscribed with The Lord's Prayer on one side, and The Serenity Prayer on the other from his pocket. He placed it in the casket beside Maxine, bowed his head and lost himself in thoughts of gratitude for her life. Placing his hand on her folded hands for the moment he said his goodbye, and as he turned toward us a simple smile of acceptance crossed his face.

I caught myself thinking back to when Jim had entered Huntington, less than two months before, and how amazing treatment and his first steps into recovery began to work in his life. It continues to amaze me how people affected with the disease begin experiencing the miracle afforded by The 12 Steps, once they've put the alcohol and drugs behind them. The "Big Book" of *Alcoholics Anonymous* witnesses to the miracle when it promises:

> *"We are going to know a new freedom and a new happiness. We will not regret the past nor wish to shut the door on it. We will comprehend the word serenity and we will know peace. No matter how far down the scale we have gone, we will see how our experience can benefit others. That feeling of uselessness and self pity will disappear. We will lose interest in selfish things and gain interest in our fellows. Self seeking will slip away. Our whole attitude and outlook on life will change. Fear of people and of economic insecurity will leave us. We will intuitively know how to handle situations which used to baffle us. We will suddenly realize that God is doing for us what we could not do for ourselves."*

I shook Jim's hand, with my other on his shoulder, "Recovery looks so very good on you." Buck gave him a friendly slap on the back.

"Thanks," Jim responded relaxed and slowly. "Max will always be part of my recovery."

"You had a special relationship."

Jim turned and looked back at the casket, "We still do, guys. We still do."

He had come such a very long way and yet there was something about Jim that continued to keep me wanting to reach deeper, wanting to help *him* look deeper into himself. It wasn't that he wanted to avoid looking into areas that needed understanding and healing, it was more that he didn't know the *wheres and hows* of his searching. There was just something about him that remained lost. I felt that Buck sensed it as well; not that Buck knew how to draw him out, but just his concerted efforts to always be there to support Jim. It was a deepening friendship that was a pleasure to watch grow.

New Years Eve was a great success. I had again agreed to work the evening shift so Dale and Rebecca could be off. Normally I would be sharing the shift with another counselor, but had agreed to work it alone, understanding that if I had any difficulties the evening supervisor at the Hospital would give me a hand. I hadn't anticipated any problems - in fact it was a bit too quiet during the late afternoon. Sarah and Maizie visited, and Maizie was on her best behavior. I was talking with Rich in the office when I saw Sarah pulling down the drive through the office window; too fast for conditions, thinking it odd she hadn't stopped in the office to say her usual goodbye. When the last visitors left and as evening approached, Peter pulled the grill on the deck out from under the snow that blanketed it, fired it up and the evening began to take on a feeling of anticipation as it led into the New Year. Wearing a chef's apron over his winter coat and holding onto a spatula as he came back in, Peter put it best as I found a fresh bottle of barbecue sauce for him in the cupboard, "Here we are, not only celebrating leaving the years of addiction behind, but looking ahead into a future of possibility that's opening for us."

"It can also be a little threatening at times, not knowing what lies ahead. You know how we like to control things, even when things were entirely out of control."

"But John, it's got to be better than what we've had."

John Aschenbrenner

- 93 -

"It *is* Peter! Our worst day sober will always be better than our best day when active in our alcoholism."

"Hey, I like that...maybe I should write that down? Got a pencil and paper?"

"Ah, Peter," I paused..."Save it for later; I think the chicken and steaks are burning, better get back out there!" He laughed, took the bottle of sauce and was off.

Both Emily the nurse and Rich the anesthesiologist - the newer residents seemed to brighten for the first time since their admission, enjoying the camaraderie of the group. Given their professions and licensing problems, they found they could relate with each other. Rich had been having more withdrawal problems than we had anticipated, and as doctors seem to make the worst patients given their knowledge of medicine and wanting to control things, he had to be reminded to leave the withdrawal protocol to the treatment team. Though he was out of any physical danger by the time he had come to us from the Detox Unit, we were continuing to titrate him down and through his withdrawal using graduated lesser doses of Phenobarbital – and he was becoming less tremulous. Rich who was in his early 40s and Emily in her mid 30s were both married with children, and their spouses were hurting and angry. Deb, our family therapist would be beginning the New Year with some difficult challenges.

I had returned to the office, checking the phone messages while the clatter continued in the kitchen as everyone prepared for the meal. Listening to the messages and making a few notes, Buck paused at the door, not wanting to interrupt but I could see that he wanted to see me. I winked, and motioned him to the chair as I took the last message and returned the phone to its receiver.

"A couple of former residents wanting to wish everyone A Happy New Year," I suggested as I turned to Buck dressed in his jeans and a navy blue Nike sweatshirt. Not a word, he nervously drummed his fingers on the desk, looking down at the floor, his right leg jumping and heel nervously tapping the carpet – reminiscent of his first admission to Huntington. Then I remembered Sarah leaving abruptly, "Buck, things aren't good, are they?"

"I don't know, John. I thought I did. I just don't…"

"Buck, you've only been back with us for a week. Take it easy. How'd things go with Sarah?"

Silence, the jumping and tapping intensified.

"It didn't go well, did it?"

"Ask Maizie!"

"Maizie? What's Maizie got to do with it?"

"She's asleep in my room," Buck looked at me like a naughty, yet perplexed school boy seeking approval for his behavior.

I frowned, "Hey I don't know if we can…"

"I didn't have a choice. Sarah and I were doing a lot of talking in my room. She got pissed and stormed off, leaving Maizie in the wake of her immaturity."

I took a deep breath, "Guess that means we won't have any leftovers from the barbecue." I tried to smile.

"I'm sorry John…but…"

"You know we can't have her here overnight, the morning supervisor is a stickler for rules, and…"

"Would you mind dropping her off at our place when you leave tonight? It's sort of on your way."

"OK, I can do that. That'll work."

"And would you…ah…would you mind…"

"Calling Sarah and tell her I'm coming?"

Buck grimaced, "It's asking a lot, I know."

"So things are more difficult again between you and Sarah?"

There was a long pause; again the drumming intensified as Buck clenched his jaw, "I don't fucking ever want to see her again!"

"Buck?"

"John, I know you guys try to hold marriages together, but it isn't going to happen. Sarah and I are through; fucking through!" His voice was determined and emphatic and carried out of the office and down the hall. "She'll always be in control, and worse yet she'll always look upon me as being less than a whole man because of my alcoholism – like I'm some amputee coming back from a war. She may as well have had me neutered!"

The sound of paws on wood floors grew closer and Maizie appeared at the door, her tail wagging, checking on what trouble her master got himself into this time! Buck's eyes began to well with emotion as he petted the lab nuzzling into his lap. "I'll fight to keep you, Maizie. You're the only family I have to care about…"

"Buck, you're shutting down, starting to feel sorry for yourself."

"*Feeling sorry* for myself?" Buck gritted his teeth and glared at me. "Feeling sorry?" Buck exhaled and crossed his arms across his sweatshirt, returning his gaze to the floor. "Fuck, I don't want to feel *anything* about Sarah. I just want her out of my life." Returning his gaze, "If I stay with her there's no way I can stay sober! *No fucking way!*"

Maizie could feel the tension, her big dark eyes looking pleadingly up at Buck. He didn't respond and she lumbered over to me, nudging my leg with her nose, prodding me to do something. I smiled at the bright animal, scratching her behind the ears and petting her as she continued to softly whimper and nudge my leg.

"I'll make a deal with you, Buck"

"Hmmm…I don't think I'm into making any deals tonight."

I paused and waited, listening to the whimpers and feeling Maizie's prodding,
"You trust me, don't you?"

After a long pause, Buck resigned himself to opening just a bit, "You know I do."

"I'll take Maizie home tonight if you promise just one thing."

"John, I don't know that I can?" He looked at me pleadingly, feeling I was about to suggest the insurmountable. "*OK,* what are you asking me to do?"

"Promise me that you won't cancel Sarah and your appointment with Deb, the day after tomorrow."

Buck rolled his eyes, looking up at the ceiling, taking a deep breath and letting it out slowly. "Oh fuck, I forgot about that…I forgot…I don't…"

"Do you trust me, Buck?"

"OK…OK…you have my word," Buck grimaced, shaking his head slowly, not believing he was agreeing to my suggestion.

From down the hall we heard the door beyond the kitchen leading to the deck slam, and Peter calling, "Peter's *best* steaks and barbecued chicken…being served!"

Maizie's ears perked, she arched her back, and looking toward the door started barking.

From down the hall, Peter called again, "Maizie, there's plenty for you too, girl!"

Later in the evening I phoned Sarah. She sounded embarrassed but thanked me for calling and that I'd be bringing Maizie home. She suggested coming to fetch the dog, but my thinking better suggested it might be best if I just dropped her off. She tried probing for information, and I gently told her it would be best to wait for Buck and her meeting with Deb.

"Then he's still agreeing to meet?"

"Yes." I felt her continuing trying to get more information, and with my not affording anything more, she thanked me saying she'd leave the light on and would meet me at the door.

After giving turnover to Carrie, shaking her head at my informing her that Maizie was in the house and that I'd be taking her home, promised me she wouldn't say a word, adding "This sure is more than a job to you, isn't it?"

"It's become the greater part of my own recovery program."

"Then you're working one *remarkable* program!"

Maizie started whimpering as I drove my Blazer up Buck and Sarah's drive. I couldn't believe how difficult it was for Buck to say goodbye to his lab, almost as if he was uncertain he'd see her again. I reassured him, though his reaction led me to believe that his mind was set on ending the marriage. Maizie led the way to the front door and Sarah let her in. When thanking me again, she took the opportunity to again seek information about Buck. Again I suggested, "You'll be seeing Deb in a couple of days," trying to leave it at that, but as I turned away I thought better, "Sarah, this isn't only about Buck recovering and getting better. This is about you getting better as well." I could see she didn't understand and wanted to take exception to my suggestions. I afforded her a simple nod and said, "We'll be seeing you soon at Huntington."

I headed home to Joanne, feeling grateful that she felt herself as much involved in my and our family's recovery as I was. We'd have our own quiet celebration, welcoming in the New Year - just grateful for each other.

It was January 2nd, and Gerry was intent on opening the first group of the New Year. "We've got a lot of *catching up* to do now that the holidays are behind us, as last week we spent much our time processing our feelings about Maxine's passing." Looking toward the most recently admitted residents and winking, "Rich and Emily have given us a good look into their lives by affording us their autobiographies which I think were excellently written and presented. You both did a thorough soul-searching of your past drinking and usage, and all of us better know the challenges you're facing." Turning toward Peter, "Peter, you asked for group time during our last meeting and we ran over with our other issues. How'd you like to begin this morning?"

Peter, not anticipating his going first, adjusted himself in his chair, leaning forward into the group and looking like a coach who was about to share a secret play with the team. He cleared his throat, looking at the others and focusing on

Gerry. "I had some difficult times during my pass home at Christmas." He paused, turning his eyes toward the floor.

Jim jumped in, "Bruno and Bertha giving you trouble in the basement?" It got the laugh Jim had hoped for.

Gerry leaned into Jim, *"And you were doing so well!"*

"Sorry Gerry!"

Peter seemed to brighten a bit, as if Jim had broken the ice for him, "Actually this has a lot to do with Bruno and Bertha. I'm thinking about changing careers - leaving the funeral business."

Jim nodded, "That'll sure make a change in Bruno's smile!" Again the laughter - Buck leading the group. Emily, Rich and the other newer members looked perplexed, as if being left out of the joke.

Buck helped out, "It's what Peter calls the corpses he's working on – a female is Bertha, and a male is Bruno…sort of vocationally-charged terms of endearment."

Gerry shook his head, again leaning into Jim, "Seems you're picking up where Maxine left off!"

This time Jim's smile was more thoughtful, "You've *got* to be kidding!" he suggested as he affectionately mimicked Max. It bought a smile to everyone remembering her overused phrase.

"I don't think I can spend the remainder of my career working with the dead and keeping a truly compassionate sensitivity with the bereaved families without posturing someone and something I'm not."

"Posturing?" Jim questioned.

"Faking it! I think I'd want to start numbing myself again, just getting through those long and lonely hours in the embalming room."

Gerry pondered the problem, "Guess I can understand what you're saying, and especially if you usually drank while doing your work."

"Somehow my work doesn't seem reflective of how I'm feeling these days; you know, more open and honest – not hiding behind my words and feelings, not creating lies that find me creating more lies to secure the original ones. And I've been thinking that there's something very plastic about how we Americans do our funerals – creating the illusion of a body looking years younger than the truth that led to death just a few days before. It's becoming too much like Madison Avenue marketing - the way we choose to deny the reality of death – by masking it behind a new suit or dress, and tons of youthful makeup."

The group grew silent, considering Peter's remarks and how reflective they were of a man looking beyond the illusions we create about life, about the fantasy castles we all build – wanting to perceive life as something more than it really is; illusions we're taught by our parents, culture and the media – the lie that life is less difficult than it actually is.

Peter reflected further, "Trying to accommodate a family whose grandmother had died after a long and physically degrading bout with cancer, I had to put the funeral on hold until I could get a Chicago Bears blue and orange casket; it obviously had to be specially ordered. She was originally from Illinois and loved the banter when the Bears were playing the Green Bay Packers, and I had to dress her in a Bear's sweatshirt and cap. I almost refused, thinking her life had meant more than what I was affording her. And selfishly I'm not sure if it helped or hindered my business, but it sure got a lot of talk around town."

Jim glared at Peter, "You've got to be kidding?" And turning to Buck, "I guess when we have your funeral we'll have to lay you out in a muscle shirt and Speedos! Don't you think, muscle man?"

"Jim!" Gerry chided forcefully, but it was too late. Jim had the group laughing and even Gerry couldn't hold back a chocked laugh.

Jim felt accomplished, having broken Gerry's therapeutic stance, "OK…OK, I'm stopping!"

Gerry returned to Peter, nodding knowingly, "Nicely put, Peter…very nicely put. I always think it's remarkable how when we begin sorting out those areas in our lives that led to or supported our addictive behaviors, we consider new avenues in life; new ways of living which we would never have considered important to our becoming sober when first entering treatment and recovery."

Rich, the anesthesiologist moved uncomfortably in his chair, clearing his throat, "I'm not sure what you mean, Gerry? I work with drugs, some of the heaviest on earth – my work is more directly related to my drug use than Peter's could ever be to his drinking."

Gerry nodded knowingly, the remainder of the group feeling the ramifications of the Rich's words. "You're saying you might be uncomfortable with the idea of returning to your practice?"

"Uncomfortable with returning to my practice?" Rich's voice grew loud and raspy, "I've spent years in med school, and years in my practice."

"I know Rich...," Gerry said slowly, affording Rich a further opening to continue.

"I...I just couldn't....couldn't start over! Tell me Gerry, you've been a therapist here for a long time. Surely you've had other anesthesiologists," and looking to Emily, "and nurses...nurses who are anesthetists. What did they do?"

"Some changed their careers, some didn't. Last year we had a doctor who changed from a long career in anesthesiology and began a new residency in psychiatry."

"What? That's insane...it...it's..."

"It's about doing *whatever* it is we need to do to maintain a successful recovery."

"OK, OK..." Rich's anxiety was accelerating, "What are the statistics for people in our careers making it after we've returned to our present work?"

Gerry paused, choosing his words carefully, and yet not wanting to sugarcoat anything. "It's not good news, Rich." Gerry paused again, Rich leaning into him, hanging on every word he was saying. "Half of those who return to anesthesiology relapse, and half of those overdose and die."

The silence in the group room was pervasive, everyone feeling Rich's tension and watching as his face turned an incredulous white. The group felt how deeply the reality of the disease had struck home, and Gerry skillfully allowed them the silence to reflect on their own vocations and life situations.

Before he lost the importance of the therapeutic moment, he added "Not only do we need to reflect on our vocations and how they might affect our recoveries; we also need to reflect on our relationships." Buck who was considering his work as an athletic trainer, thought himself in the clear. Gerry's final remark cut deeply and the group very quickly picked up on his grimacing and the cadence of his nervous knee.

Jim, sitting next to him, elbowed him gently in the ribs, "You OK?" Gerry catching his concern and Buck's sudden nervousness focused his attention on Buck.

"I'm OK. It's just that when you mentioned relationships, I'm reminded that Sarah and I have a session with Deb this afternoon."

Gerry nodded and used Buck's comment for the group, "We all have our challenges. Some are workable and some aren't. There are no easy answers. Situations and relationships affect each of us differently. There are no set rules, but one thing is always clear; we need to advocate for ourselves and our individual recoveries. Recovery has to remain our number one priority – without it we are no good to ourselves, the people we serve, and the people we find ourselves in relationship with."

Peter nodded knowingly to Gerry, "I guess that says it all. I'm sure I can't go back into the lonely, present a phony-image-of-caring, put your best display-of-a-body-with-a-smile out there mortician's life."

"Have you thought about what you might like to do, what new career you'd like to pursue?"

Peter looked at each member in the group, and shrugging his shoulders, "I think...I think I'd like to sell cars."

A short moment of silence and Buck and Jim looking at each other burst into laughter, Jim falling off his chair and onto the floor blurting out, "You've *got to be fucking kidding me!*"

Gerry shook his head, "Peter, we need to talk!" He dismissed the group early for lunch, suggesting Peter remain behind.   After lunch Buck's disposition turned pensive, with him avoiding his peers and spending time alone, trying to read but finding himself staring out the windows, reflecting on his marriage. At 4:00 Buck climbed the steps to Deb's office on the second floor. Deb had thought it best for Sarah to meet her there, allowing for Buck to avoid any confrontation prior to the meeting. If there was to be a confrontation, it was best that it happen in Deb's office.

Deb always dressed so professionally. She looked confident and yet very compassionate sitting at her desk, in her black business suit with red pin-stripes and piping, a matching red lace blouse and complementing lipstick and nail polish completing the look that was always Deb's mark of affording her clients respect and the best she could afford them. In recovery herself, she held a healthy regard for herself which reflected in her continuing hope for her clients. Sarah, dressed in a very pretty and feminine light blue sweater to match her eyes, and a jean skirt fidgeted nervously, readjusting herself in the comfortable upholstered winged armchair.

Buck entered the room, determined and trying to believe he wasn't feeling anything, and greeted Deb. He looked matter-of-factly at Sarah, affording a simple "Hello," and looking away took the matching chair near her, his eyes focusing on the floor, fingers slowly drumming the fabric of the chairs arm.

Deb got to her feet and out from behind her desk, and with a note pad took her place at a smaller and comfortable chair in front of them. She began softly, "Buck, you and I have spent a short time together, and Sarah...you and I've talked briefly on the phone since our last meeting. Other than what I already know we need to consider, given the difficulties you both had on New Years Eve, I think we might begin by talking about Buck's recovery as well as what that means in terms of your marriage, and to talk about how both of you might consider viewing things differently now that Buck is in recovery. Things won't be the same – can't be the same as they were, and I think you both have some sense that's true. Buck has had to begin looking at life differently and has made great strides in those areas. We still have a way to go here at Huntington, and after discharge we encourage our former residents to view recovery as a life-long process. So, with that, Buck let's start with you." Deb shifted in her chair, leaning toward Buck.

"Why are we starting with me?" Buck looked defensively at Deb, "I only agreed to this meeting because I gave John my word I'd meet. I truly don't see the point of this."

Deb started to respond but Sarah broke in, grabbing the arms of her chair and arching her back, "Buck, I'm here trying to save our marriage and you're not even wanting to..."

"Wanting to *what* Sarah; try to save *our* marriage? Don't you mean *your* marriage?"

"That's really stupid, Buck?"

"Is it?" Buck glared coldly into Sarah. "You don't want me. You want the *illusion* of a perfect marriage. You want to parade me around like some trophy you were able to catch – that stud athletic director at the gym! And what guy would mind that, except that you want nothing more than to control that image of a husband...want nothing more than to control me, and recreate me in the image of what you want me to be!" Buck fell back into his chair as if he was glad he had finally said what he did; that it was out there."

"A trophy? *You, a trophy?*" You're *quite* the trophy! Parade you around...*parade you around?*" Sarah was on her feet, mimicking locking arms with someone who was at her side, "Look everyone, here's my stud of a husband – here's Buck; the falling down, pissing on himself drunk, and you know what Buck?" Sarah was standing directly in front of him leaning over and getting in his face, "They tell me you'll *always* be an alcoholic – that you'll *never* be normal again." Sarah was trembling, backed away and fell back into her chair, tears falling down her cheeks. "Some...some trophy! Here's how someone in Al-Anon put it to me: 'He's crossed the line from being a cucumber, becoming a pickle – and *once a pickle* there's no turning back to being a cucumber!'" Sarah was almost spitting her words. "There's my trophy stud husband – a pickle! *A god-damned shriveled up pickle!*"

Buck reddened in anger at the illusion to his manhood, breathing deeply - nostrils flared, gritting his teeth.

Deb tried to diffuse the explosive tension. "Sarah, you mentioned Al-Anon. You've been to a couple of meetings?"

"Yes, I've gone." Sarah was trying to compose herself, "Gerry had mentioned it to me when he called suggesting Buck and I start meeting with you. I've been there twice."

"Was it hard going the first time?"

"I didn't know why I was going, other than Gerry telling me I should. I don't have the problem – He does!" She pointed her shaking finger at her husband. I met John's wife there, and she's convinced me to keep going. I'm still not sure I should be..."

"I think it's so important for you to continue going. You'll learn a great deal about the disease, how it's a family disease, about your relationship to it, about acceptance..."

"*Acceptance?*" Buck blurted. "Sarah will *never* be able to accept my alcoholism – she's just like my father and would rather find another way around this – medication or whatever. I think she'd rather I had cancer. Maybe she'd be able to *feel* something about that. Her friends would understand *that*! And what's this stuff about Al-Anon and acceptance?

I heard a guy joke about how people in Al-anon define relapse among *their* members." He leaned across and into Sarah. "*A moment of compassion'* – fits you like a glove, Sarah! *Compassion?*" Buck reared back as though in disgust, "Well, you can take your fucking shriveled pickle and…"

Deb intervened, raising her voice, "Buck, that's not true about Al-Anon. My husband continues to go to Al-Anon and I know how it's helped us strengthen our marriage. AA, Al-Anon and keeping the lines of communication open. We've grown closer because of it all."

Sarah and Buck grew silent, like two prize-fighters taking to their separate corners, Buck gripping the arms of his chair and Sarah biting her lip with eyes searching the ceiling, feeling her world closing in on her – her not being able to control it. Deb allowed the silence, if not for anything other than for the couple to catch their breaths and try to refocus. More moments passed. Deb, about to break the silence, looked at Buck seeming to relax in his chair - loosening his grip and looking out the window, decided go give him a bit more time.

Buck would admit to me later in the week that a curious feeling seemed to come over him during those moments when looking out the window and beyond the turmoil. In the midst of the confusion he thought to something we often repeat at Huntington:

*Serenity
has less to do
with avoiding the storm
than it does
with maintaining one's calm*

*in the midst
of the storm.*

Buck considered it, thinking he didn't have anything to lose and that his only other option was to return to his rage and eventually storm out of the situation – his usual way of reacting. Buck took a deep breath, searching into his being for his sense of his Higher Power while continuing his gaze through the window into the winter sunset, feeling himself not only surrendering his own control, but into the powers beyond himself.

Deb watched him curiously; watched him relax - his shoulders dropping and Buck falling deeper back into his chair. She understood, and smiled, nodding knowingly. Buck caught her eye and simply shrugged his shoulders. More moments passed, Sarah continuing her gaze at the ceiling.
Buck inhaled deeply, and continuing to rest his head on the back of his chair turned toward Sarah. His words came slowly and softly.

"Sometimes…sometimes I feel like I'm expected to perform like I *am* at the gym – to know the perfect moves, the perfect way of being, to be the perfect this or that – that there's no give and take between us; nothing to understand and nowhere to be understood. Sometimes Sarah…" Buck paused, choosing his words carefully, his eyes welling in emotion, "Sometimes late at night when I'm closest to you…I…I feel…I feel the most alone." Buck returned his gaze out the window.

Sarah stiffened, gritted her teeth and turning to Buck, "How *dare* you! How dare you talk like that about our marriage? It *could have been* the perfect marriage, like all our friends thought it once was."

Deb couldn't let it pass, beginning gently, "Sarah, Buck is talking about how he feels. Right now he's not challenging you about anything. He's talking about how *he* feels. It takes us a long time here at Huntington, and he's worked very hard to begin to relate to his feelings. Many of us drink because we felt we needed to repress our real feelings, and as we continued to deny or numb them through our drinking or using, we eventually began to lose all connections to them. We found ourselves in a world devoid of feelings; in a wasteland – a flatland. Buck's feelings are his. We can't tell him they're not, or that they're wrong. They are what they are, and they're real."

"My Buck – the stud, *feeling?*"

"Getting real, Sarah, finally getting real," Deb continued to hold her eyes on Sarah.

"I don't know if I'd know who he is? Sure wouldn't be the guy I married?"

"In many ways, when a spouse goes through treatment and is in a
successful recovery, it's like starting over."

"Starting over? Us, starting over?" Sarah turned toward Buck, "Can you imagine that, *us* starting over?"

Buck returned his focus to the room, first toward Deb and then to Sarah, "I don't know if I can either?" His words were soft, almost resigned to the uncertainty of what he was feeling. Again silence filled the small office.

Deb feeling they had reached deep enough during their session, quietly began, "How about the three of us closing here, but you two continuing this for awhile longer?" Both Buck and Sarah looked at Deb uncomfortably. "I'd like the both of you to leave Huntington for a couple of hours, to go and have dinner together before you return home, Sarah. But I have some ground rules for your time together. Talk about anything, especially about how you feel; talk about anything except for a few things. I don't want you talking about alcoholism, Buck's treatment, or expectations on either of your parts. Talk about friends, about Maizie, about anything else. It's sort of a *time out* for both of you – a time to just *be* with each other. Think you can do that?" She looked at both of them. Buck nodded, as did Sarah, if reluctantly. Deb formed a T with her hands. "If either of you begin talking about what you're not to consider, give the other the *timeout* sign."

Buck reached across to Sarah's chair, putting his hand on top of hers. At first Sarah tried to pull away, but steadied her hand under Bucks, putting her other hand atop his. Getting to their feet they thanked Deb, Buck following Sarah out of the office and down the stairs to his room to fetch his coat.

When they were gone, Deb closed her office door and dropped back into her chair, resting her head and closing her eyes - contemplating her own grateful sense of surrender to The Powers that uphold us all. Moments later she reached across to her desk for a book of writings, a book of spiritual reflections written for therapists in recovery. Opening it to a dog-eared page she had nearly memorized, she again read:

"We all love the metaphor of coming home. It's why the airports, train stations, and highways are crowded during the holidays – not so much to be celebrating any specific day, but to again fulfill that need to travel the journey we find within our souls - to take those seemingly endless steps on the highways and byways toward our own homecoming -until our final spiritual homecoming is achieved. And where best in our lives to meet this need for a deeper metaphor reflective of our spiritual completion, then to enter the doorways provided in the day-to-day; to enter through the archways provided by those we love – a mate, a spouse, a lover – to share in that special being; becoming one in that being. It moves the metaphor to a higher level – the highest level of our need to describe the celebration of our eventual reunion into

The Power that continues to fathom this universe."

Deb closed the book, grateful for her work with recovering people – those recovering through their own personal struggles, and those close to them, learning to live life differently through their relationship together. Again Deb felt the gratitude for how her work supported her own recovery. The days passed, with Buck and Sarah again meeting with Deb later in the week.

Another cold mid-January Friday morning found me climbing the front steps to begin my AM shift with Buck meeting me at the front door, opening it for me. Feeling the warmth flow out to draw me in, Buck's smile seemed just as welcoming.

"Can I buy your coffee this morning?"

I was amazed how relaxed Buck seemed, "Only if you can find two extra large mugs, and you'll have the other with me after I take turnover from Carrie?"

"You bet!" He headed toward the kitchen and I found my way into the office.

The night shift turnover was short. Although the night was quiet, Peter's wife had visited during the PM shift, and she was being resistive to his making a career change, especially given that he was entirely uncertain about what he might be doing. Emily's husband and children had visited and things seemed to go well. Rich had had an explosive conversation with his wife on the pay phone, causing Rebecca and Dale to become involved and ending the call, and something seemed to be eating at Jim who was becoming more unresponsive as the week ended. I promised Carrie I'd try to have a word with him. Turnover complete, I helped Carrie with her coat and headed toward the lounge, following the smell of fresh coffee and finding Buck in comfortably worn jeans and a faded and frayed red sweatshirt, sitting in front of the windows watching the sun rise and doing a few bicep curls with a 20 lb. dumbbell he lowered to the floor as I entered.

"Staying ripped?" I smiled his way.

"Ripped? I'm just trying to get some tone back, or I won't be looking much like a trainer when I get back to the gym." Buck's words held a warm and quiet modesty.

"Something tells me you're not going to have much trouble."

"We'll see about that, John. I'm not eighteen anymore."

"Don't *even think* about going there! Twenty-eight, and you're worried about your virile years being over! I *don't* think so!" I took a chair across from Buck as he handed me the hot coffee and I afforded him a reflective smile. "Buck, I'm a bit uneasy about us meeting here again. It was a morning just before Christmas when we were here and you told me you were leaving. I'm hoping you're not..."

"Not even close...I just wanted to talk about somebody...somebody who seems to be looking at things differently these days." A long pause followed, Buck surveying the landscape of his own thoughts.

"Is it Sarah?" I jumped in; certain that's where he was headed.

"No, although she's part of it," Buck paused, almost seemingly embarrassed, and nervously fidgeting – his eyes avoiding mine. His mood became markedly more serious as the silence became almost ominous.

"Then it must be Maizie?" I smiled, trying to lighten the moment.

Buck smiled and again becoming serious stared at me momentarily before responding. "It's my father."

I suddenly grew as serious as Buck, remembering the trail of devastation the last time Buck's father became involved in his treatment.

Buck reached into a front pocket of his Levis, pulling out a folded note, and just as quickly reached for the section of a week old newspaper on the table. Holding onto both,

"John, something hard to explain happened yesterday. I was rummaging through this old newspaper that the cleaning lady forgot to get rid of, and you know that nondenominational spiritual column in the second section?"

I nodded, knowing it featured different faiths and denominations.

Buck pointed to the column, "It's talking about forgiveness, and then includes the story of the Prodigal Son, from St. Luke's Gospel." Buck slowly began to read:

"...While he was still a long way off, his father saw him and was moved to pity. He ran to the boy, clasped him in his arms and kissed him.

Then the son said, "Father I have sinned against heaven and against you. I no longer deserve to be called your son."

Buck's eyes filled with emotion and he choked on his words, looking to me, then back to the folded newsprint, continuing:

But the father said to his servants, "Quick! Bring out the best robe and put it on him; put a ring on his finger and sandals on his feet. Bring the calf we have been fattening and kill it; we will celebrate by having a feast, because this son of mine was dead and has come back to life; he was lost and is found." And they began to celebrate..."

Buck let the paper drop to the table, and reached for the folded note, handing it to me, not unfolding it. "As I was reading the biblical quote, the morning mail came. It's from my father."

Before I opened it I shook my head, trying to find my own words of caution - trying to protect Buck from the...

"Just open it, John."

I did.   It was a simple hand-written note, on his father's professional letterhead, featuring his father's embossed, *Dr. Robert Jaeger M.D. – Psychiatrist.* Written were the simple words:

Buck, I've been such a fool. Can you find it within yourself to forgive an arrogant man's insanity? I love you son, Dad.

Included with the note was the same *Prodigal Son* newspaper clipping Buck had found in the paper the housekeeper forgot to throw out!

The room went silent. Both of us reached for our coffees, sipping the brew and looking out onto the snow-drifted garden. The moments passed, and Buck shifted in his chair, "Sarah said she wants to start dating again."

Confused, not certain what he meant, Buck immediately picked up on my discomfort.

"Me! ...Sarah wants to start dating *me* again!" Buck reached to steady his quivering jaw. Sarah and my father have come such a long way to..."

"Buck!" I stopped him, "*You've* come such a long way, and you're bringing them along in your journey. They're following your lead."

"Following *my* lead?"

"You're again affording the portal through which they again can see how much they love you. You've opened the door, Buck. All they have to do is come in.

"Coincidences, John?" Buck questioned, wanting to again hear my response, the response he knew and felt."

"No coincidences in recovery Buck! *Miracles*...always and again, just miracles.

VII

With Eyes That Know the Darkness in My Soul

If courage and surrender are the pillars by which we practice and encourage others to approach their recoveries, acceptance is the bedrock upon which those pillars stand. For most alcoholics and addicts, before entering into recovery, reality is the proverbial difficult pill to swallow. We tend to feel that life should be pain-free, our spirits should always be elevated, that we should be more handsome or beautiful, richer and more famous. Nowhere in the equation is the cold fact that life is, by its very nature, difficult. Once that reality is accepted and truly integrated into one's expectations, an amazing thing happens – life is no longer difficult. *It is what it is!*

Driving home on a late afternoon as the sun was setting I realized again how the cold and early darkness that ends January days continues to take its toll on me. Knowing how much I enjoy the music of the 60's and 70's, Rick had given me a Don McClean CD for Christmas. As the remaining daylight cast its' long shadows across the snow-covered fields, McClean was strumming his guitar and singing "Vincent," a wonderfully imaged ballad on the brilliant perceptions of Van Gough – a sadly misunderstood and under appreciated artist. Something in the words *"...with eyes that know the darkness in my soul,"* made me think of Jim and how reclusive he'd become. I had tried to give him as much space and time as I thought healthy, but when Gerry also indicated his frustration at Jim's distancing himself during group, I felt it was time for some gentle confrontation. Tomorrow was Saturday and I was working an AM shift. Weekend mornings were usually quiet with residents sleeping in as long as they could before the scheduled meditation. I'd make a point of seeing him.

Jim always slept in on weekends, usually just making it to meditation, but in the past week he seemed more anxious and was up early, first making the coffee for the house and then making himself scarce. I found him in the lounge – in his worn baggy sweats, hands in the pockets of his hooded sweatshirt, and though dressed in his most frayed attire he was meticulously groomed, as always - not a hair out of place. The TV was on but Jim, not paying attention, just stared off into the distance of his anxious thoughts. He turned toward me as I walked in and was pleasant though guarded when I said, "You look down lately, what's going on?"

"A lot on my mind," he responded, shutting down the possibility for a conversation and then becoming increasingly more evasive, the more I attempted to engage him.

"Gerry tells me you've become less responsive and more defensive in group and even Buck has said…"

Jim glared at me, cutting me short, "What's Buck got to do with this? This doesn't have a god-damned thing to do with Buck!"

"Whoa…I'm just trying to say that Buck is concerned about your…"

"Well let's keep Buck out of this." His voice accelerated as he again avoided my gaze, "He has *nothing* to do with this."

"Jim, I'm just trying to…" Coincidentally Buck walked into the lounge. Jim looked at both of us, got to his feet and nervously brushed past.

"John, I'll talk to you later."

I couldn't just let it go. "How about we meet sometime before lunch in the office?"

Jim afforded an exasperated "You can find me when you want me," almost as if he had just entered treatment, continuing to wallow in his defensiveness. He disappeared down the hall.

"What's that all about?" Buck felt as though he had violated our privacy. "I didn't mean to…"

"It's not you, Buck." I looked at my watch. "Hey, I'm losing track of time. You and I are late for morning meditation! You're supposed to be keeping me on track, Buddy!"

Buck laughed, "I'm supposed to be keeping *you* on track?"

As we left the lounge, I slapped Buck on the back, "Gerry and Dr. Segen tell me that you're getting close to discharging."

Buck grew serious, "And I'm not sure I should be going; I've been getting nervous. I'm hoping we can talk sometime today. I've got some things I'd like to ask…to talk with you about, if you have time."

"I'll find the time Buck, though it might be a bit later. I want to talk with Jim and I'm admitting a new person right after Meditation. That OK with you? But for now I'll meet you in the group room. Tell the others I'll be there in a minute."

Buck agreed and I went to the office to collect the morning meditation book we always use, thinking about the conversation with Jim and his odd reaction. Over the past week it seemed the closer Buck and Sarah were becoming in their relationship, working through their issues, the more distant Jim was becoming to Buck. In the past Buck would use Jim as a sounding board to work through his issues with Sarah, but recently when he tried Jim would shut down. Buck even tried confronting him in group, and, to Gerry's dismay, Jim became even more anxious and defensive.

Jim said as little as possible during the meditation, trying to avoid me on the way out. I headed toward the office where I found Terry from Admissions with the new resident. The young man looked nervously at me, his eyes filling with emotion. "They say I'm getting better. It's slow, but I'm getting better." His voice was raspy and he looked as if I were judging him, having the authority not to admit him. "I…I truly *want* treatment."

Terry looked somewhat apologetic. "John, we're sorry we didn't give you more advance notice, but Joe has come to us directly from a two months stay at University Hospital in Madison. You can review the paperwork for yourself, but in a nutshell, Joe's 34. He's a Professor of British Literature at The University of Wisconsin now on health leave. Joe admits to being an alcoholic, and has been sober these past two months while in the hospital. I guess it's pretty obvious that he's had a rough go of it, and is still facing some difficult health challenges, trying to slowly bring his body back to…to…well, to where it's functioning normally. He's had some expert care, and when Dr. Segen called us this morning, he indicated that in his phone discussions with Joe's Madison doctors, they almost lost him a couple of times. He's a fighter and somehow his liver continues to try rallying, and now that he's somewhat stable, they suggested he *try* a residential setting where he can begin getting treatment for his alcoholism. We can manage his medications here at Huntington, but as Dr. Segen explained to Joe when he talked with him on the phone, it'll be a day-to-day and see-how-it-goes situation here at Huntington. Dr. Spiegel will be here on Monday morning to see Joe, and said he wants to spend a lot of time with him, evaluating how he's feeling and how the weekend went."

I put out my hand and Joe gave me a nervous handshake. I tried to muster a smile, but remained overcome with the sight of the physical devastation caused by the disease. Joe was remarkably thin, a handsome man from the cut of his features, though emaciated to the point of looking like an Auschwitz prisoner on The History Channel, his skin the color of old yellow oak varnish, and the whites of his eyes the color of a yield sign. I thanked Terry who headed back to the main hospital, and offered the unsteady man an office chair.

Just then Jim appeared at the door, impulsively blurting "John, I want to apologize for…" when he saw Joe. "Oh, I'm…I'm sorry, I didn't mean to…"

"It's OK Jim. I'd like you to meet Joe, our newest resident. I'm just checking him in."

"Hi Joe," Jim offered him his hand.
Joe tried standing but just as quickly fell back into the chair, "I'm sorry, guess I'm still a little weak from my hospitalization and the trip here…I…I"

"Hey, not a problem," Jim said guardedly, not wanting to say the wrong thing, swallowing the lump in his throat.

Jim focused on me. "Just wanted to apologize for how abrupt I was, and I think I'd like to spend that time with you, when you can."

"I'll come get you, Jim. OK?"

"When you have the time; looks like this guy needs you right now more than I do." Returning his attention to Joe, "Welcome to Huntington, and let me know if there's anything I can do, or for that matter, what any of us can do for you. It's a great bunch of people you'll be sharing this house with." And pointing toward me, "And *great* staff; any problems, come to this guy. If it wasn't for him I would have bolted out of here a long time ago."

I felt somewhat embarrassed. "Hmmm, you must be wanting something," I winked, "I'll find you when Joe feels at home. OK?"

Jim left and I continued with Joe's admission, doing the necessary paperwork and having him sign the required forms. He grew tired quickly, losing his attention, his signature getting shakier and almost unintelligible. Sitting at the side of the desk, he kept his left hand at his side, fingering something as the minutes passed. Suddenly he dropped what he was holding, bending over to retrieve it from   the floor. It was a rosary. That was odd, I thought. I knew many Catholics, myself having been brought up in a very orthodox home, and now not avowing any structured organized belief, feeling myself even more spiritual because of the break – but I hadn't seen a rosary in years; even among the catholic priests that we had as residents now and again. Joe returned to fingering the beads, and I noticed his lips silently forming the prayers as his fingers moved from bead to bead.

"Are you Catholic, Joe?"

"I was born a Catholic, dropped away, and while in the hospital I was visited daily by an old retired priest who made it his business to visit the sick; himself a recovering alcoholic. I guess if one considers having a sponsor in recovery, he's the nearest I've come to having one."

"And you pray the rosary?"

Another man might have been embarrassed by the question and the invasion of what might have been private in his life, but Joe wasn't. "I don't know how much I acknowledge the prayers, but it keeps my anxiety level down. It keeps me occupied and the demons of my Angst at bay." He looked at me anxiously, as if the mention of his fears found him again facing the death he had courted over the past months.

I didn't know what to say, and just nodded my understanding. "I haven't had a chance to check over your medical paperwork Joe, but given your difficult condition, do you mind my asking how much you drank?"

"I've been drinking heavily since I was 29 – so, for the past five years, ever since I became a professor. Guess there wasn't anything more for me to strive for, and I tried settling into my life but it was just never enough, and I started drinking. In the beginning it was just enough to numb myself during the evenings, and as my tolerance increased I drank more and more, until I was drinking near a liter of vodka a day."

I understood what he was telling me, though others not finding themselves faced with dependency issues might not. The underlying nature of the addictive personality is an obsessive-compulsive nature. The obsession for Joe was his insatiable need to strive toward ever higher goals. First it was his Bachelors degree, then the Masters followed by his Ph.D. Once his achievements were attained and there was nothing to obsess after he became depressed and anxious – the obsession and it's compulsion wanting to find an avenue for its energy. It was all too easy for him to dilute the anxiety and depression with alcohol – basically why workaholics become alcoholics when they retire.

"But Joe, you're only 34 years old. We've got people who drink that much for decades before they face what you're facing." I shouldn't have looked so perplexed; I knew the answer, but had never *seen* the hard reality of how devastating the disease could be at an early age.

"It happened suddenly. I started eating less and less, and my body started shutting down. I couldn't believe it either, and started questioning my doctors. They told me that all bodies metabolize alcohol differently, and each liver is different in its short and long term ability to continue functioning." Joe looked down at the floor, "I guess I'm one of the unlucky ones."

While I carried Joe's bags to his room, he used the restroom, because I had given him a urine cup for the necessary lab specimen. He met me in the room, handing me the closed container and asked if it would be OK if he slept for awhile. I told him I'd wake him for lunch, suggesting that I'd bring him a tray from the kitchen rather than have him walk over to the main hospital with the others. Somehow I knew he'd sleep thought his lunch. Returning to the office I looked at the urine specimen. It was dark brown, the color of old leather. I had never seen another specimen like it, and my heart sank deeper as I suddenly realized just how physically compromised Joe's health was. Quickly I paged through the sheaf of admitting papers that needed to be assembled in his chart, looking for the latest lab work from Madison. I found the results of his Liver Panel screening, and his most recent GGT, the test for liver enzymes. I stared at the results, holding my breath. A normal GGT ranged from 0-50. His was 3000. I checked the date of the test – it was from blood drawn just two days prior. Joe was in deep trouble.

While putting Joe's medical chart together in some reasonable semblance of order, Emily came into the office for her morning antidepressant, "Sounds like Buck might be discharging within the next week or so. Jim's going to be lost without him."

I glanced up at her. "You wouldn't guess it from the way Jim's been acting, hardly acknowledging Buck this past week. I know he thinks Buck is working a strong program of recovery, and you'd think he'd be happy that he's getting close to discharge; that he's learned what he can here and..."

"I don't think it's about Buck's recovery or that he's discharging," Emily paused, washing down the medication with a Dixie cup of water, "I think it has more to do with Buck and his wife's relationship having improved."

"What?"

"Just a woman's intuition maybe, but I think Jim's feelings for Buck go beyond friendship."

I pushed the office door closed, almost angry at her suggestion. "Emily, before you got here Jim came very close to having to leave because of being in bed with a female resident who *did* leave because of it. You've heard that!"

"I know. John, maybe it's nothing and I really like Jim and hate to see him so bent out of shape. I worry that he might be thinking about leaving treatment. It's almost like he wants to deal with something that he's not able to face. And whatever it is, Buck's relationship with Sarah seems to be forcing the issue."

"But how could *you* think you'd see that in Jim?"

"Because my younger brother, who I dearly loved and who everyone thought was the biggest stud about town shot and killed himself. I found him the next morning, an empty brandy bottle and a suicide note – his telling us that he couldn't bring himself to let us know he was gay."

I grimaced at Emily's telling, feeling the pain she continued to hold, "And you think that..."

"I know it, John. I can feel it. Jim and I've talked about my brother's suicide and about the things he couldn't face. But it's not something any of us are going to easily confront. It will be devastating for him if he's not ready to explore it on his own."

"I agree, but we can at least afford Jim a comfort level in which he might begin to explore those feelings, and..."

The front door opened and just as quickly slammed with a crash. Heavy snow-covered paws thundered down the hall toward the office. Maizie tried stopping at the familiar office door, landed on her hind quarters and slid past with a yelp! Emily and I watched the raucous display and I found myself laughing so hard I started coughing. It was almost surreal, like the comic relief one sometimes finds at a funeral – enough to cut the pain.

I couldn't hold my exuberance, "Maizie, Maizie...go find Buck! Go on, go find Buck." She didn't need to be prodded; sticking her head into the office and making certain he wasn't with us, "Go on Maizie, find Buck!" She continued down the hallway to Buck's room, pushed open the door and jumped up on him, just as he was pulling a sweater over his head, knocking him to the bed and landing on top of him.

Sarah sheepishly came to the door, looking exasperated, "Honestly John, I tried! I tried getting her on her leash after I opened the door, but...well..." Sarah looked at me like a naughty girl. "Guess it's time for Maizie and I to get Buck back home, before Maizie gets her own posse of hounds and takes him hostage."

Laughing I suggested, "Sarah, Buck's recovery sure is looking good on you these days."

Initially Sarah didn't know how to respond, and then nodded, "I've never felt more hopeful, and I haven't been this happy since when we were first married."

"I know, it shows. It shows on Buck too."

"Thanks John. You don't suppose I could spring Buck for lunch, do you? Maizie and I thought we'd take him out. I've packed some sandwiches and a thermos, and thought he'd like to go for a hike with us."

"I'll bet you could! You know where to find him!" Sarah left and in a few minutes the three of them, ready to leave, passed the office door, Buck sticking his head in.

"John, I'm still hoping to have that talk."

"How about we try when you get back?"

They were off, and I returned my attention to Emily, looking for holes in her thinking, "But how do we explain his being in bed with a female resident?

"My brother always tried to play it straight. I learned in grief counseling after his suicide that especially when it comes to the addictive personality, sex for the sake of sex can be common regardless of the true object of one's desire, but that in recovery it becomes amazingly more difficult when one focuses on being true to one's real feelings."

"Was your brother a recovering alcoholic?"

"He didn't go through treatment, but tried to work a good program following AA principles. He went to meetings and tried to work The Steps. When approaching his 5th Step, when he was to spill his guts to his sponsor, it became too much for him."

"You're saying he could no longer continue the lie?"

"He didn't know he was lying? He had built a fortress of denial around his homosexuality; not allowing himself to be able to see it, and when he did it was too late. I think if he had been nurtured within the safety of a treatment setting like Huntington, it may have been different."

I felt the pain of her loss, "I'm truly sorry, Emily. It must have been…"

"Hard? It almost destroyed me. I'm having such a difficult time just sitting by and seeing Jim go through this." Emily wiped her tears with a Kleenex she pulled from the box on my desk.

"You *really* believe that Jim is gay?"

"I'd bet my recovery on it!"

"Whew, let me see what I can do, what inroads I can make without directly confronting him. But I'm guessing if he does come forward with this new awareness it might be with someone like you; given what he knows about your brother, he might consider you having a better understanding. He might think you to be his safe haven."

Emily left the office, and I checked the clock – another hour before lunch. I left the stack of unsorted paper on my desk, checked on Joe who was sleeping soundly and entered the TV lounge where I found Jim half-heartedly watching The Sports Channel. Looking up, he nodded and seemed to brighten. "I hope you're not pissed off at me?"

I shrugged my shoulders, "How could I be *pissed* at you Jim? What do you say we go into Dr. Segen's office where we can have some privacy?"

"OK, guess I could use some of your *stellar wisdom.*" Jim tried to smile, and was trying just as hard not to become defensive."

We walked to Dr. Segen's office, and I closed the door behind us, offering him the large leather desk chair, "You play *big guy* for awhile," I said, taking the padded side chair. Jim didn't argue, sat down and struck an anxious pose, leaning back in the doctor's chair, wearing his ragged sweats, nervously fidgeting his fingers on the padded leather arms. I didn't say anything, thinking Jim was expecting some sort of confrontation given his recent behavior. When the confrontation didn't come, he seemed to relax, almost as if he were trying to surrender his anxiety.

Jim began slowly, "We talk about this being a program of honesty."

I could feel the difficulty in his words, and replied softly, "Yes we do."

"And I've heard you say that when it came to recognizing your alcoholism, you were the proverbial *last one to know.*"

"I couldn't allow myself to recognize what I feared were my deepest failings?"

"Failings? What about your deepest feelings?"

I eyed Jim curiously, sensing him dig deeper. "Feelings?"

"When you got sober, when you got *real*, were there feelings you found surfacing that you couldn't believe you had, feelings you felt you *shouldn't* have?"

"There was anger; there were resentments."

"And you could deal with that?"

"Not entirely, not all at once; but in time and with the increasingly greater degree of acceptance that arose from my ability to *turn my difficulties over* to my Higher Power – well Jim, I can *promise* you it gets easier."

"And what about those things you couldn't believe you were finally recognizing, those things that you repressed under increasing amounts of alcohol?"

I remained silent for a moment, nodding my understanding. "It sometimes gets difficult, especially when we find we've been living a lie, and finding ourselves at the same time appreciating the honesty we find ourselves longing for; reveling in that feeling of freedom as we recognize and acknowledge each new discovery about ourselves."

"Can it ever be too large a discovery; too much to handle?"

"That's when we can be fortunate we're in treatment with a group of people who are here to support us, who are here to nourish our honesty – to encourage it."

Jim crossed his tensing arms – his fingers digging into his sides, his breathing becoming more anxious. "You always seem to know just the right thing to say."

"You're a good man, no matter what you find surfacing inside you, even if it seems to turn your entire world upside down. In reality you're beginning to turn your world downside up. It's about getting real Jim, no matter what that reality is."

Jim paused, "But what if it's just *too* big?"

"We're only as sick as our secrets, especially those secrets we keep from our true selves. They gnaw at us until we can't help but return to the alcohol or the drugs to again suppress the pain."

Jim's eyes began welling up. He kept his arms crossed, biting his lip and sobbed. I reached across and handed him the box of Kleenex. He didn't reach for them, allowing his tears to flow. "I can't…can't go back there again, John. I jus…just can't."

"I know. I'm just hoping you might be able to…"

Suddenly there was a hard knock on the door, coupled with Emily's anxious, "John, John, are you in there?"

I reached for the door knob and opened the door. "Emily, what's…."

"The new guy, Joe…he collapsed in the hallway." I flew out of the room, heading down the hall with Jim and Emily on my heals, reaching Joe – just trying to pick himself up off the floor outside his room. I reached him as he stumbled again, grabbing one arm and Jim reaching for the other to steady him.

"You OK, Buddy?" My words were loud, revealing my own fear and need to be certain that Joe was able to focus on me.

Joe was exhausted from the effort. Jim's own anxiety, as he saw the jaundiced face of where he could be headed if he didn't embrace the most essential aspects of his treatment became too much for him. He broke down again, sobbing. Joe, not understanding tried calming Jim with a weak, "Hey, it's…it's OK…I'll…I'll be OK, just got up too quickly I guess. *It's* happened before. His eyes met Jim's, looking perplexed. "You sure *you're* OK?"

Emily, sensing what was going on put her arm around Jim's shoulder, "Let's see if we can find some place to talk," Jim didn't need to respond and followed Emily into the lounge. She closed the door behind them. I helped Joe into the office, took his blood pressure and other vitals. He seemed to be stable, but I called the RN House Supervisor, erring on the side of caution. She suggested I keep an eye on him and that his vitals should be taken every four hours. Joe and I continued to talk and just as I was about to walk him back to his room so he could lie down, Emily stuck her head into the office. "Do you think it'd be OK if Jim and I went to the village for lunch?" Jim was standing behind her, somber and in control; his eyes would not meet mine.

I thought for a moment. We didn't allow a male and female resident off the grounds on their own together unless there was a third person, but before I could suggest the obvious, Emily looked at me knowingly, and winked "It'll be OK, John. Trust me, it'll be OK!"

"Hmmm," I groaned, biting my own lip, thinking that given Jim's history with *hot pink* Angel on Thanksgiving, any administrator would call me to task for my obvious lunacy, and yet knowing what I knew, suggested uneasily, "I guess it'll be OK. Be back before the next shift arrives. Can I hold you to that?"

Emily nodded and Jim's eyes finally met mine, allowing me a timid and exhausted, "Thanks, John."

The remaining residents began to file past Joe and me as we were heading back to his room, on their way to the main hospital dining hall for lunch. As Peter passed, I called him back, "Could you do us a favor and bring a lunch tray back for Joe, our new resident - after you finish with your lunch?"

"Sure, so you're the new guy

"Peter this is Joe; Joe this is Peter." They shook hands; Peter like the others was momentarily taken aback by Joe's jaundiced appearance and apparent weakness.

"Hi, what do you do, Joe?" trying to get past his own awkward need to stare.

"I'm a Lit Professor at UW-Madison," Joe said cordially, "What do you do?"

Peter froze, feeling the gravity of Joe's compromised condition, and stammered, "I...I...well...right now I'm between jobs, looking for a new career," and wanting to change the subject quickly, "I...I'll have your lunch back here soon. Are you...are you...ah...you hungry?"

"Just some light stuff, OK?"

"OK," and with that Peter was out the door with the others.

I helped Joe back to his room, telling him that when he got up the next time to either get up slowly or call for someone. He assured me he was feeling better and sat at his chair at the desk, saying he was going to review the handbook I had given him.

Returning to the office, I tried to catch my breath and process what was going on, as I poured another cup of coffee from the pot and grabbed the sandwich I had brought from of the refrigerator. Seeing Joe's urine specimen on the door rack didn't help my appetite. It wasn't the specimen that bothered me. We were always meticulously careful where in the fridge things were placed, sealed in the tagged bags – it wasn't about the specimen, it was about the gravity of Joe's compromised health. Sitting in my office chair and unwrapping my tuna on rye, I paused, looking out the windows at the frozen gardens, thinking about Jim's struggle to get entirely honest with himself, Emily's reliving her brother's suicide, and Joe's all too apparent image of what happens when alcohol gets close to winning the battle. Again, the words from Don McClean's ballad began filtering through my mind, *"…with eyes that know the darkness in my soul."* I needed something positive to focus on, something that was alive and healthy, something that was honest. As I began reaching for a meditation book to seek out some inspiration, I heard the front door open. I felt grateful for the familiar footsteps approaching the office. I could feel Buck's broad, relaxed smile fill the room even before he entered. I pushed the book aside, "Trust me, Buck…you're a welcome sight for sore eyes!" Buck eased himself into the chair.

"You OK?"

"Things just got a hell-of-a lot better!"

Buck frowned, not fully comprehending, "Sarah and Maizie are on their way home. We had a great hike, but I told them I wanted to talk with you before you left for home."

"I suppose you're going to tell me your leaving – going AMA; that you've had it with this place."

Buck smiled, "Funny thing…now that Gerry and Dr. Segen tell me I'm ready to discharge and get on with the world out there, I'm nervous about leaving."

"A bit of nervousness is a healthy thing, keeps us on our toes during those first few days as we settle into a new routine. But there must be some excitement…?"

Buck nodded, "I'm very excited, thinking about starting over with Sarah. Even though things got rough for us, she stood by me. She's agreed to go to Al-Anon, and we've agreed to see a marriage counselor to work on improving our ability to communicate with each other. I suggested it and she readily agreed."

"*You* suggested a marriage counselor? Think about where you've come, from when you and Sarah had your first meeting with Deb, when you couldn't care less if the marriage lasted."

Buck looked at me seriously. "John, I love her deeply. She's become such a big part of my support system. She recognizes her co-dependency in my drinking and is beginning to understand the role she played. Though drinking isn't an addiction for her, she's choosing to abstain; says it's really not that big a deal for her; that she'd do it for me."

I smiled, "So when's the big day? Have Gerry and Doc given you their blessings with a date?"

"Tuesday at the end of our group session; they want to both meet with me on Monday afternoon and make certain there aren't any holes in my aftercare plans, and I'm to give them a schedule of my intended AA Meetings and their locations. They also want to summarize things for me. Deb said she'd try to arrange her schedule to take part in the meeting."

"I'm so very happy for you." I reached out my hand and Buck took it, and rather than shaking it and letting go, he just held on.

"I ah, I need to ask you something, John." Buck searched the floor and then the ceiling, his blue eyes filling with emotion, finally letting go of my hand and wiping his eyes with his sleeve. "Damn, I thought I could do this without all the drama."

I couldn't resist the opportunity, "And forget about how you've learned to feel what you're truly feeling?"

Buck sniffed back the tears, wiping his eyes again, "I…I'd like to ask you if you'd…ah…" Buck refocused on my eyes and paused, "I mean… I'd be honored if you might consider…consider being my sponsor."

It was my turn to feel the emotion. I reached for his hand again, held it and covered it with my other. "I'm the one who's honored. Of course I will."

"I…I know it's a bit unusual, given staff – resident boundary issues, but Sarah and I approached Deb who asked Dr. Segen and Gerry, and of course they agree. Sarah trusts in you as much as I do, and has really gotten to know Joanne at the Al-Anon Meetings." I could feel Buck's excitement as he continued to ramble on."

"Meeting might be a bit of a problem though, but I'm sure we'll work out some sort of a schedule to…"

"Hmmm, I've considered that too," Buck sported a sly grin as he reached in his pocket and handed me a laminated card.

It was a year membership to the fitness center where he worked as a trainer. "It's as close to your house as it is to mine, and on the way to Huntington, and besides…" Buck patted his hard mid section as he pointed to mine, "I might be able to help you with that middle-age spread!"

"*Middle-age spread?* What middle-age spread? We both laughed. "Well, OK, I guess I could use some work."

"*Some* work? I'm just hoping I haven't cut off more than I can chew here! Don't want this to interfere with my recovery!" Again, we laughed.

"Thank you Buck, It'll be a good way to continue into this New Year. I'll bet there are a lot of things you'll be able to teach me!"

Growing serious again, "Not as much as you'll continue to teach me, John; I'm so very honored."

"We'll make quite the team."

"You bet we will."

Then I got serious, "Now can we talk about something else!"

"You're my sponsor, let's talk!"

"This is difficult, Buck. It's about Jim."

"I know; something's been up with him for awhile. I've tried to talk with him about it and he avoids me even more. I try to give him his space and yet he almost seems angry with me. I don't get it."

"He's going through some really rough times right now, and there are some things that are amazingly tough for him to face. I think today could be a pivotal day in his treatment – either he deals with what he needs to deal with, or I'm afraid he might bolt out of here."

Buck's tone was serious, "Where's he now, John."

"He's in the village with Emily having lunch."

Buck looked at me curiously, almost as if I were adding another piece to the puzzle in confirming something he suspected, "But why would you let him go to the village alone with a female? You'd never let another guy here get away with that?"

I stumbled on my words, "Because, well…because I think there are issues in Emily's life that might help Jim face what he needs to…"

"Her brother?"

I must have looked like a deer caught in a cars headlights, "How would you…?"

"Jim's been interested in my relationship with Sarah from the beginning, and the closer Sarah and I came to finding ourselves, the more distant he became."

"How could you be so perceptive to guess that…" I stumbled on my words, not wanting to break any confidences, whether real or imagined. Again I tried to reword my question, "Buck how could you guess that Jim…"

"Is gay?

"We don't know that entirely. I mean he hasn't…"

"I know. Where do you think I've been these past two months?" Buck smiled comfortably. "I've been learning to relate to other people's feelings as well as my own. At first I thought I was imagining it, given Jim's early morning rendezvous with Angel on Thanksgiving, but I've had a couple of experiences with guys who have tried to get too close at the gym when I was giving training sessions. It was all very innocent at first, and I'm sure Jim didn't have a clue where he was going with his feelings."

"I *can't believe* how perceptive you are, Buck! You really amaze me."

"You've been a great teacher!"

"Buck, you picked up on Jim's feelings long before I did."

"But I was the one who…" The front door opened and Peter came into the office with a covered lunch tray, placing it on the desk in front of us and backing out, thinking Buck and I were having a personal one-on-one.

"Thanks Peter. I guess I'd better get this to Joe."

Buck eyed me curiously, "Who's Joe?"

"Our new resident; come on, I'll introduce him to you, but…" I tried to warn Buck, "Joe's facing some serious physical difficulties; he's in pretty bad shape." I picked up the tray and Buck followed me to Joe's room where we found him sitting at his desk, his head in his hands and nodding off, trying to get through the handbook.

"Joe?"   I   said   softly.

He turned to me, "Almost made it through the reading materials"

"How about some lunch, it's still warm?" I placed the tray in front of him. "I'd like you to meet Buck. Buck's been here about two months and is nearly ready to discharge."

Trying to stand and then thinking better, Joe extended his hand and Buck took it, feeling himself looking at what might have been if he hadn't gotten treatment when he did. "Having a tough go of it?"

Joe gave a half nod and then shook his head slowly, trying to smile. "I'm going to do this!" he said weakly.

Buck tightened his grip, his voice filling with emotion, "I'll help you in any way I can. We all will."

I encouraged Joe to leave the remainder of the reading until tomorrow and to join the others in the TV lounge where he could get comfortable on the couch, and just relax during the afternoon. He had done enough for one day. He said he would and thanked us. Buck and I headed back into the hall as the front door opened; a teary-eyed Emily and a half-smiling Jim entered, stomping the snow from their shoes. Not intending to encounter either one of us as quickly as they had, they both eyed us cautiously, almost curiously. I invited them to use Dr. Segen's office if they wanted to continue their talk. Jim said he'd like to talk with Buck and me. Emily smiled and suggested she'd see us all later and continued down the hall.

Entering the office I closed the door behind us, each of us taking a side chair and avoiding the large desk chair. I felt the need to break the ice, "Did you and Emily have a good lunch in the village?"

Jim avoided the question; as if he didn't need an opportunity to begin, "You both know how difficult it's been for me over the past weeks."

We both nodded.

"I think it was so difficult because I didn't entirely know what I was feeling, and gradually when I thought I did...well...I didn't know if I could face it." He focused on Buck, "And I've treated you the worst of all - Buck, I'm truly sorry for that."

I cautiously tried to soften Jim's words, "When we finally get down to where we're feeling our true feelings, they're sometimes hard to define, and our reactions aren't always intended to hurt or to alienate."

"What I found was that since I was an adolescent I've been alienating myself from my true self. When I saw Joe today, I realized I couldn't continue the charade, or if I did I'd end up more compromised than he is – that I would surely die from this disease." Jim paused, holding onto the words he had just expressed. Buck and I afforded him the space to feel, nodding in agreement, again suggesting we understood his struggle. "And then...well...John it was almost as though you led me through the darkness to where I could again see the way. You showed me where the road led...and well...Emily gave me the final courage, through her telling me of the challenges her brother faced. She helped me look into my darkest corners, and open the closet door I found there, and here I am, stepping out into the light."

Buck understood the metaphor, got up and pulled Jim to his feet. They both embraced. When Buck stepped back, I stepped forward, "I'm so very proud of you Jim...so very, very proud of you."

Jim stood, smiled, and tried to focus on Buck, "And it doesn't matter?"

"I'll just be careful not to drop my soap in the shower!"

Jim looked stunned for the split second, until Buck's smile broadened across his face. "It truly doesn't matter that I'm gay?"

"Not at all, one of my best friends is!"

"You never told me you had a friend who was..."

"You still hadn't recognized it!"

Buck embraced Jim again, offering to help him sort through the ramifications of his insights, encouraging him to try to focus on each day as he entered it, and not to look too far into the future – practicing his surrender to his Higher Power and approaching life one day at a time, not becoming discouraged, and when he felt the burdens were too much, to reach out to those who would understand – those who would help support him.

As we left the Docs office, I caught myself thinking that courage doesn't always roar – that most often, true courage is that silent voice at the end of the day that says 'I'll try again tomorrow.' I went to check in on Joe, hoping he'd be allowed the same opportunity in recovery – the time to heal and win the battle against his own demons.

VIII

Flying

Tuesday came quickly for Buck – too quickly. I heard him coming down the hall, singing the words to R. Kelly's 1998 hit, "I believe I can fly," and sounding like he shouldn't give up his day job to become a soloist. But he didn't care. His words grew louder as he got closer.

"*I believe I can fly. I believe I can touch the sky. I think about it every night and day, spread my wings and fly away. I believe I can soar. I see me running through that open door. I believe I can fly...I believe...*" Buck turned into the office.

"Sounds like your ready to leave this nest," I suggested as he grew silent, and a bit embarrassed, looking like an innocent kid just off to interview for his first job, dressed in navy blue pants and a button-down pin-striped shirt. "You look like you're ready to take on the world."

Buck smile broadly, his blue eyes bright and animated, "I was feeling a bit shaky this morning, wondering if I really *am* ready. What do you think?"

"You *know* you are, and a little nervousness isn't necessarily bad. I'm nervous too, thinking about having to start working out at your gym!"

Buck laughed, "Trust me, I'll take it easy with you – hell, I need to get myself toned up as well. It's been awhile."

I reached onto the desk and handed him a photo. "I want you to have this. It's the identification photo we keep in the medication book that I took when you came in."

Buck looked incredulous as he stared into the eyes of the pained and angry face that stared back at him from the two month old photograph.

I watched him intently, "You were begging me to teach you how to drink socially – Your words, *Just fucking teach me!*"

"And then you told me you understood, that you had been there, that *you* were in recovery."

I nodded.

"So, how about joining us in Gerry's group this morning? If you can break away from the office, I'd appreciate your being there as I say my goodbyes."

"I don't know if Gerry would..."

"I already asked him," Buck paused, "So you're coming?"

"Guess I don't have a choice! Wouldn't miss it, Buck!"

By 10:00 the residents had all clambered down the stairs to the large group room, Buck looked like an anxious school boy as he took his seat next to Jim – both seated across from Emily, Joe, and the others. I took a chair next to Joe and waited for Gerry, who finally came in with Peter – both preoccupied in what appeared to be a serious exchange; Gerry not liking what he was hearing.

Gerry took his seat next to Peter, welcoming everyone to the morning group, and finally turning his attention to Buck. "Today's an exciting day for all of us, as we'll be wishing Buck good luck on his leaving us, transitioning back home and to his life in recovery beyond Huntington." Gerry paused, collecting his thoughts, gently slapping Peter's knee. "But before we focus on Buck, Peter needs to talk about a decision he's made and I hope he might remain open to our suggestions and opinions regarding what he has to tell us." Gerry slapped Peter's knee again, and then sitting back in his chair, gave Peter the floor.

Peter reddened, cleared his throat, and began slowly. "I hadn't planned on coming into group this morning." He paused, looking embarrassed. "I thought I could just meet with Gerry and be on my way. But Gerry convinced me I owed it to you all to tell you what I've decided." Peter looked about the group and nodded, "He's right, I owe you all a great deal." He cleared his throat and then focused on the floor in front of him, not wanting to see the group's reaction,

"I'm leaving today. I had a long talk with my wife last night, and although you think she's controlling the outcome of my treatment, I'm deciding to go back to my work at the funeral home. We live there, and the owner will have me back in the business – in fact he's begging me to get back as soon as I'm able. He's tried a new mortician who isn't working out. I know this last stage of my treatment has to do with rebuilding my life vocationally and well … now that I'm going back into the same work and my boss is expecting me to be back as soon as I can get there, I've decided to discharge today and…"

"Don't do it, Peter!" Buck began slowly and then leaned forward in his chair, his voice becoming louder and more agitated. "Don't do it! You've come so far, and now you're backing down and into an *easier way*.
There *are* no easy ways in recovery. You *know* what we say each time we read *"How it Works,"* when we begin an AA Meeting… *"Half measures availed us nothing!"* This isn't about taking the easy way out. It's about doing whatever it takes to insure your recovery.

"That's easy for you to…"

"*Easy* for me to say?" Buck was on his feet. I nearly died of this disease, and so did you. *All* of us are here at Huntington for that precious chance to make it out there. Turning toward Joe, their eyes met and Joe nodded his agreement – Buck wanting to reflect on Joe's jaundiced struggle to regain his health, but no longer feeling the need because it was so very apparent, returned to his passionate plea with Peter, "Don't do it Peter. Don't go back into those basement work rooms where it'll be all too easy to hide your booze behind your embalming fluids. Your recovery needs to work some other way…it needs to…" Buck paused, tears running freely down his cheeks and onto his shirt. The group watched intently, nodding in agreement. Joe closed his eyes, fighting back his own tears. Buck continued, "Your recovery needs to be *your* recovery. Not your wife's idea of what your recovery should look like. It needs to be what you…"

Peter was on his feet, cutting Buck off in mid-sentence, his face red in anger as he looked toward the group. "I have to go," he said abruptly turning, and headed toward the door. "John, I'll meet you at the office after I've finished packing." The door closed behind him, and a heavy cloud fell over the group. Buck took his seat; a dejected look filled his face as he gripped the sides of his chair. For moments, nothing was said, Gerry allowing what had just happened to sink in.

Jim finally broke the silence, "We've got something to celebrate today here at Huntington, and I want to be the first to wish Buck well as he accepts the challenge to live a life in recovery beyond Huntington. Turning his attention to Buck, "I for one am going to miss you, Buck. I don't think I'd still be here if it hadn't been for you, and I know I wouldn't be dealing with my true and deeper issues if it hadn't been for you and Emily."

Buck smiled, nodding humbly. "We'll stay in touch, Jim. You can trust me on that. Your recovery has taught me a great deal. Your courage in being able to relate on a *feeling* level teaches me so much about that emotional level I need to relate from in my own recovery, and especially with my wife and intimate friendships." Buck got to his feet, crossed the room and embraced Jim in a tight hug. "I have no doubt that you'll lead a remarkable life in recovery; not doubt whatever."

Gerry began slowly, trying not to focus on Peter's decision to leave and sensing the groups understanding of the gravity in his impulsive move, "Jim's absolutely correct, and has made a great start in what we need to do this morning. We're here to reflect on Buck's recovery, and to afford him closure to his treatment, and any words we'd like to send with him. Buck's asked John to join us. Although it's a bit unusual for someone who's on staff at Huntington to sponsor a resident, given that they're both in recovery and live close to each other, and their wives have become friends, Buck has asked John to sponsor him – and something tells me it's going to be a great relationship." Gerry looked my way. I smiled and nodded in agreement.

And so it continued, each member reflecting on Buck's accomplishments in treatment – those difficult moments he transcended through his newfound spirituality, and those pitfalls that sometimes turned around into bittersweet moments of tears followed by the laughter. When everyone had shared their thoughts, Gerry got to his feet, reaching into his pocket.

Buck, having been at other closing meetings of former residents, got up from his chair, smiling shyly, clasping his hands behind his back, "Gerry, I'm feeling nervous about leaving. Although I've waited for this day, I'm feeling a bit unsure that…"

"You're ready, Buck! I have no doubt that you've received all the tools you'll need." Gerry pulled his hand from his pocket, holding onto the shiny, heavy brass token, engraved with the Huntington Logo on one side, and a thematic verse Huntington has been giving its residents since it first opened its doors years before, on the reverse:

*We
bring about
new beginnings
by deciding
to bring about endings.
To renew our lives
we must be willing to change,
to make an effort
to leave behind
the things that compromise
our wholeness.
The universe rushes in to support us
whenever we attempt
to take a step forward.
Anytime we seek to be
in harmony with life,*

to make ourselves more whole,
all the blessings
that flow from God
stream toward us,
to bolster
and encourage us,
because all Life is biased
on the side
of supporting itself.

Gerry turned the token to its inscription and handed it to Buck, "As our tradition here at Huntington requires, before you leave with our token, you need to share its words with us.

Buck began slowly, all eyes focused on him, his words a bit shaky, "We bring about..." He started, tears beginning to flow down his cheeks. He wiped his eyes with his pin-striped sleeve, took a deep breath and continued. As he neared the end, he paused, looking about him, not a dry eye in the circle, "And everyone, I love these closing words. There were so many times I just held onto them, trying to get to the next moment, to the next hour, '...*because all life is biased on the side of supporting itself.*'
You've all taught me so very much, and don't think you're getting rid of me so quickly. I don't live far, and will be back to visit. Hell, I'll challenge any of you to a game of Trivial Pursuit on any weekend you'd like!"

Joe, who's color was looking better today, was the first to respond, if weakly, "And don't forget to bring Maizie with you!"

Buck and the group laughed heartily, "For sure, Maizie will be with me, Joe! You can bet on it!"

An excited and beaming Sarah was waiting for Buck upstairs, Maizie by her side, sniffing out the excited emotions being displayed – Sarah almost unable to contain her, handed the leash to Buck. Jim and even Joe helped Buck with his bags. Buck protested, telling Joe he'd get them. Joe wouldn't hear of it, said he was feeling the best he had in a long time. I followed them to the door, Buck telling them he'd meet them at the car. There was a freezing mist in the air, and I found myself telling Buck to be careful driving, like some kid I was sending off to college. He dismissed my words, as if he didn't hear them. His thoughts were elsewhere.

Buck put Maizie's leash in his left hand, extending his free hand to me. I took it, his grip firm and tight. It wasn't enough; he pulled me into a tight hug. "I...I couldn't have done this without you, John."

I stumbled in my response, "Just...just remember Buck, I may have more recovery in my past than you do, but when it comes to the present and future, I don't have a second more!"

"I have such a hard time understanding how we found each other, how the winds of fate have been so generous to me."

"What are you talking about? You said it yourself?"

"What? What are you talking about?"

"Life is biased on the side of supporting itself!" I smiled, slapping Buck on the back. "It was meant to unfold this way."

"So, I'll see you tomorrow at the gym? I'm starting back there tomorrow morning and after checking with Joanne, I've taken the liberty of making an appointment to meet with you at 4 o'clock, after you leave Huntington"

"Ugh..."

"Hey, you can't..."

"I'll be there...I'll be there!"

Finally jealousy overcame Mazie and pulled her master out onto the front steps; Buck catching himself slipping on the new-forming ice.

"Careful, Buddy, I don't want you in a cast tomorrow as you're teaching me how to get pumped." Buck smiled broadly and winked as Maizie pulled him around the corner.

It had been a long morning. My attention returned to losing Peter, and meeting Gerry back in the office I told him how difficult I thought it would be for him, returning to his old work setting.

"John, I've watched many people come and go through these doors. Some of the people we hold the greatest hope for, people we are absolutely certain about *making it* out there, don't. And then there are those who we think have only the slightest chance of maintaining, and they do marvelously. There are so many variables involved in a recovering person's life, and though I agree with you about Peter, only time will tell."

"And Buck; what are you thinking?"

"Buck truly wants his recovery. It's so apparent. He'll have his challenges, but I'm one to believe that to the extent an alcoholic wants and is willing to work for his recovery – to that extent he'll have that recovery. As far as your being his sponsor, consider it a blessing. You and I know what 12th-Step work means to our own recoveries. He'll be a challenge for you, but he'll also help you secure and enrich your own recovery."

"I know Gerry. I know!"

The temperatures dropped as the afternoon found me leaving work. The icy mist turned into snow, and the trucks were out salting as I headed out Huntington's driveway in my Blazer, putting my transmission into 4Wheel drive and heading toward the main road home. I had decided to stop at the local sporting goods store, needing some new gym shorts and shoes if I was to begin working out the next morning. Thinking about what a great trade-off it would be for me to sponsor Buck and for him to be working as my trainer; I caught sight of the old brown farm truck to my left, trying to stop at the crossing I was entering. He hit his brakes, and slid through the stop sign and into the intersection as I slammed on my brakes and tried to...

The last thing I remember was the crunch of metal into metal, the searing pain in my mid section...and the darkness.

It's a funny thing about life - it seems that for the general public it's appreciated most after it's been threatened or after one comes back from some life threatening illness. Talk to a cancer survivor and they'll tell you how great it is to see another sunrise, another sunset. Talk to someone in recovery from alcoholism or any of the other addictions and they'll tell you the same, and yet they'll note a difference. For the survivor of a physical illness, they'll talk about having avoided death, and how appreciative they are for being given a second chance. After they've completely recovered they seem to slip back into their former focus and approach to living, until something happens again, and then again. The recovering alcoholic or addict views things differently. They tell you that they *were* dead and that continuing recovery provides them with a daily reprieve from a disease that lays waiting for them, eagerly anticipating their relapse and return to drinking or using. The recovering person marks success only with each new day well lived, approaching merely one day at a time and allowing those days to add up on their own into a lifetime lived in grateful recovery, reveling in each and every sunrise and sunset, living life on life's terms…even when life presents itself as an old farm truck barreling though the intersection.

Darkness opened to a nauseous and cold haze, with EMT firefighters barking orders to each other. The pain was excruciating, and I dropped off into the darkness again - and that darkness opened into a feeling that I was flying, and then floating like a rudderless boat adrift on an endless sea. Darkness and time became one, and often fell off into nothingness to return only to the darkness and feeling of floating.

Words began begging me, words mixed with emotion and the beeping of machines; Joanne's voice, Rich's pleading and all of it too quickly falling off into only the beeping, rushes of pain and the darkness once again. Perhaps it was a minute, maybe a day, maybe years; I heard Buck's voice. I heard Jim and Joe's voices seeming so near and yet so distant, taking about Peter's death. I wanted to ask, wanted to talk and finally I tried…feeling my distant lips moving.

"John?" It was Buck's excited voice. "John? Are you with us, Buddy?" I felt a hand clench mine, and again the darkness, Buck's voice fading in the distance.

Again the silence opened into the sound of distant people. I opened my eyes. The beeping was gone. I was on my back, propped up in a hospital bed finding myself staring at a triangle-bar grip positioned above my chest. My legs were spread wide under the sheets, a foam barricade keeping them separated. I tried moving my right and then left leg, feeling the dull pain and heaviness in my hips. My left hand was taped to a board, a bag of IV fluids dripping into my veins. Before I drifted back into the darkness, I remembered the brown truck. I felt the distant tears; heavy tears of fear – fear of the unknown.

The darkness opened into the feeling of Joanne's hand gently stroking my right hand and arm. Before I opened my eyes I braced myself, remembering my legs, the IV drip and the hanging triangle. I opened my tear-filled and frightened eyes, focusing on Joanne, deep in thought. "Jo…Joanne," I whispered.

"John!" Joanne jumped, her hand gripping mine. She saw the agitation I was beginning to feel. "It's Ok…it'll be OK, John. It'll be OK."

"Wha..what…?"

"You had an accident, John."

"I remember the ice…the…the brown truck!"

Joanne squeezed my hand tightly in both of hers. "It'll be OK, John. The doctors say they're hopeful that you'll make a good recovery."

I looked down at my legs, still separated by the foam divider. "What happened to me?"

Joanne paused, collecting her thoughts. "During the winter, you…"

"During the winter; what do you mean, *during the winter?*" This is still…

"It's the beginning of March, John. You've had a bad concussion, and have been here these past 6 weeks."

"But...but...what about my..." I looked down at my legs.

"You're lucky to be alive, John." Joanne fought back her tears. "The accident broke both your hips and you've had replacements. A therapist has been in here twice a day massaging and working those new joints. They say they're happy with your progress. Although your muscles are weak, they're saying that with some expert rehab you'll be walking again soon.

"Rehab?" I choked on the word, confused and thinking..."
"Don't worry John," her smile forced the first laugh she'd probably had in weeks. "You're still sober!"

I felt myself smiling, squeezing Joanne's hand. "Well *thank God* for that!"

"I'm so glad you're back. Rick and I thought we were losing you."

"I don't understand...where's the time gone?"

"The doctors say it might have been a mixed blessing. Though you're muscles are weak even with the therapy you've been given, your wounds have healed and you shouldn't have any more incision pain – maybe just a lot of tightness. And there'll be a lot of muscle pain – and the physical and emotional frustrations in learning to walk again. You know how you can get. We've been waiting for you to come out of your coma so you might begin to do those things. I'm hoping your doctor and surgeon might be coming in today. They both want to talk with you, and then we'll set up a program of rehab."

I tried to move my leg, trying to pull myself up.

"Use the triangle bar." Joanne pulled it toward me.

I grabbed onto the bar with my right hand, and then my left. My arms felt heavy, weak from disuse. I fell back onto my pillow, feeling a cramping in my legs.

"Let me raise the bed," Joanne pressed the remote, and saw my look of helplessness. My head was beginning to pound with pain."

"John, this is going to take a long time. It's going to take a lot of work, and you'll be OK with that, but you've got to go slow and just focus on this day, and then the next."

Another familiar face entered the room, "You know…just like working *our* program – one day at a time, one step after the other!" Welcome back, John." Buck took my hand, pulling me into a firm hug!

I relaxed, needing to hear those simple words…*one step, one day at a time.* My headache subsided and somehow I knew I'd be OK. I realized I'd have all the support I needed – from Joanne and my recovering friends.

"Buck, how…how have you been? You look great." And he did! Wearing a slate blue cotton sweater, his shoulders were larger and more defined and his chest broader and biceps bulging through his sweater – eyes clear and his smile proud. I said it again, "You look *great!* I can see how well you're working your program!"

Joanne put her hand on Buck's shoulder. "Buck and Sarah have called every day, have come over to the house and have helped me with things while Rick's been away."

"Looks like I owe you, Buddy!"

Buck's blue eyes moistened and he wiped away a tear on his sleeve, silently shaking his head in disagreement.

Joanne couldn't resist. "Don't know what I'd have done without him. He kept telling me that a guy like you couldn't leave us – that you were too strong, that you're will was too determined, regardless of whether you were conscious or not." Joanne pointed to the chair in the corner on the other side of the bed. "Buck often spent long and late evenings sitting alone here in the room after I left. One of the nurses said she thought he was Rick's older brother, finally sending him home when the night shift came on."

I looked incredulously at Buck. "You did *that*, Buddy?" Buck shrugged his shoulders as if it were nothing.

"What about a sponsor Buck? You had just left Huntington, and Joanne tells me I've been out of touch for over 6 weeks. You were just heading out and it could have been a difficult transition time for you. Did you find a sponsor, Buck?"

Buck whispered his response, his voice shaky. "I didn't need to find one, John. I just needed to *wait* for you. You *helped me save my life,* John. There were just a couple of very difficult moments, and I just...well...I just did the next right thing, and when that got near impossible, I...well..." Buck paused, trying to collect his next words.

"What Buck...*what* did you do?"

Buck shrugged his broad shoulders, "*I came here.*"

I didn't try to hold back the tears.

Buck's voice became more controlled and more forceful. "Was it you or me who said, 'We're going to make quite the team?"

"I...I don't re..."

"I do. It was *you.* And I'll tell you what else is in store for you. I've talked with the physical therapist when he's been in here working your legs and new hips. They're going to get you up and walking here in the inpatient rehab program, and then they're turning you over to me! I've already worked it out with my manager. You'll be coming to the gym, and we'll do the work we need to do...and gradually we'll work into a training program. You'll be good as new before you know it! Your surgeon says there's no reason you can't make an entirely complete recovery."

I smiled helplessly, knowing Buck's plans couldn't be more thoroughly considered. "So, what about your AA Meetings? Have you been going to your meetings? You know how important..."

"I promised you and the folks at Huntington I'd get to a meeting each day for at least three months. I have to apologize that I've been making six meetings a week...and on the other day...well..." Buck paused.

"Buck, what about the seventh day? You know how we feel..."

Joanne jumped in, smiling warmly at Buck. "John, that's the day he'd sit here late into the evening, reading out loud to you - from The Big Book or from his meditation books."

I choked on my words, "What...what a team!" I sighed.

"What a *coach!*" Buck whispered.

"Hmmm...we'll see who the coach is when you're barking orders to me at the gym!" I winked.

The following day I told Buck I remember having a dream about Joe, Jim and him talking about Peter – that Peter had died. "It must have been all the narcotics I was receiving when I was unconscious. How are those guys doing?"

Buck grew serious, "It wasn't a dream, John. Joe and Jim and I were in your room – it must have been two weeks ago. It's true. Peter is dead."

"What? Ah, Jesus...was it an accident...did he...?"

Buck tried to choose his words, but there wasn't any way to sugar coat it. "At Peter's wife's prodding, he returned to the funeral business, and was going to meetings in the area for a couple of weeks and then it seemed he suddenly dropped out of the recovery scene. People tried contacting him and he wasn't returning the calls. Then...well...very quickly it turned bad for him and was too late. I picked up Joe, Jim and Emily, and we all went to the funeral."

"*What* happened?"

Buck paused, "His wife found him in the embalming room, an empty vodka bottle on the counter, and Peter on the floor with a pistol in his hand. There was a simple note lying on the table. It said he'd rather be dead than going back into the bottle."

My stomach sank, "I'm sorry I wasn't there for you, Buck."

"I needed you most on that day. I was here that night until Sarah called the hospital and the night nurse found me sleeping in the chair, The Big Book in my lap. It was that night Sarah and I truly realized what a horrible disease alcoholism is. She got me home and we fell asleep crying in each others' arms. It was then she understood how much your friendship and sponsorship means to my continuing recovery."

"How are Jim and Joe doing?"

"Jim is getting close to discharging, and Joe? Well, Joe is looking great. Wait until you see him. His color has returned, and he's intent on joining us at The Mt. Olympus Gym!"

The hours moved into days. The first days were difficult with the physical therapist and often Buck helping me out of the bed and positioning me behind my walker. First a few steps, then more, and more. The exercises were excruciatingly painful in the beginning, with the nurses reminding me to call for my pain medication an hour prior to my scheduled time in the physical therapy room, on the therapy bed and mat. Buck called it my workout session, and in many ways it was. He became as much my encouragement as did the physical therapist, and in many ways given my addictive personality – sensed more quickly how to deal with me, sometimes needing to slow me down, where a therapist would usually be finding himself encouraging his patient to do more. There were the leg raises, hip stretches, the hip adduction and abduction exercises, riding a stationary bike, learning to climb and descend stairs, learning to get in and out of a car, relearning to do such simple things like getting dressed and putting on socks and shoes – first with gripping and pulling aid devices and finally as any normal guy would accomplish the seemingly simple tasks. Frustration would set in, and somehow when things were darkest, I'd get a call from Buck or he'd stop in and would know exactly what I was thinking. His 'easy does it' and reminding me to 'live life on life's terms', or even just his usual *knowing nod* was enough to revitalize me, to put me into a better frame of mind, to help me keep going. 'Progress not perfection,' he'd say, and I'd take another step, even if a faltering one.

Buck had started attending my usual Tuesday night meeting at a local spiritual retreat center, and my friends there decided to bring a couple of meetings to my hospital room. They were great meetings, people sitting around the room as I rolled about in my wheel chair. The nurse didn't question the congestion, just shrugged her shoulders and smiled my way.

After another week of physical therapy and my giving up the wheelchair entirely for the walker, my surgeon told me it was time to go home. The next day Joanne came to pick me up, just as Dr. Schultz again dropped in to wish me well and arrange my follow-up appointment.

Joanne eyed him curiously, "Doctor, John tells me you told him he could drive as soon as he feels comfortable, and that he can go to the gym." I could feel her concern, her fears.

The doctor smiled. "John's been a model patient. A double hip replacement is quite an accomplishment for me as a surgeon, but mostly for him. It's a very rare situation to have both hips replaced in one operation. It's been John's determination that has taken him this far, and which will take him into a complete recovery. Though there have been some frustrating moments, John's never complained about the effects of the accident. He's done everything we've suggested and more. I've never *ever* had a patient like him. His attitude and insight in approaching rehab after surgery is unprecedented, even in a patient having a single hip replacement. The physical therapist tells me he can effectively fold his walker and hop into the dummy car we have in the therapy room. He's quite capable and is very careful in responding to his environment." Dr. Schultz looked at me questioningly, "And who's the guy who's been helping you out?"

"You mean Buck?"

"Yes, the young guy. He stopped me in the hall the other evening, asking me about working with you at the gym. He's quite the friend. I asked him a few questions and shared a few simple recommendations about working with a person with replacements. He entirely understands the physiology and the precautions he needs to keep in mind when working with you. And John, I have to tell you, he thinks the world of you. He told me you've helped save his life, and that he's so grateful to be able to help you in any way he's able. What happened? You save him from drowning?"

I shrugged my shoulder, "Something like that, Doc!"

"Anyway Joanne, John can drive as soon as he feels comfortable and yes, he can go to the gym when he feels he's ready. I think he has a fairly good understanding of his limits, and if he doesn't his body will tell him soon enough. He knows about the precautions to avoid dislocation, and his physical therapist says he's done a nice job demonstrating how careful he needs to be until those leg muscles, ligaments and tendons are again taught enough to do the entire job for him."

Joanne eyed Dr. Schultz suspiciously, "You *do* know how obsessive John's addictive personality can be!"

Dr. Schultz laughed, "It can be his downfall, but in this case it can be a remarkable asset if John is careful and uses his obsessive nature in a positive way. John and I have had many talks, and I have to tell you, he's an inspiration to me. He's agreed to come speak to new patients facing surgery."

Joanne winked my way, "He's an inspiration all right! Some days I could use a little less of his inspiration!"

I laughed and so did the doctor, knowing full well what Joanne was saying.

"I'm keeping John on a pain patch for a few more days and I'll write a script for some pain medication that doesn't have too much risk of dependency, but knowing how John feels about pain meds and addiction, I'm guessing he won't have it filled. He can use Tylenol for the tightness and muscle pain he might continue to feel for awhile, and I'd suggest he take it before heading to the gym."

The doctor left and Joanne helped me get dressed; Levis and a comfortable sweatshirt. "Do you know how good it feels to have jeans on again?" I buttoned the waistband, amazed at how much weight I had lost because of the surgery; my increased metabolism focusing on my bodies healing. "Guess I won't have much more weight to loose at the gym."

Joanne eyed me curiously as I reached for my leather jacket. "Promise me you'll go slow John. You've lost a lot of muscle tone, and it's going to take awhile for you to get back in shape. Truthfully you could use a few *extra pounds*. I've already had my *little talk* with Buck and he's agreed to keep an eye on you."

I gave Joanne a kiss on the forehead, "I'll be careful, Honey. I love you so very much." Zipping my jacket I reached for my walker, positioned myself behind it and grabbed the rubber grips. We walked to the elevator, and entering, waited as the doors closed on yet another chapter of my life. Leaving the Lobby, and on the other side of the revolving door I found a springtime fresh with a cool mist-laden air and green grass. Daffodils and tulips were blooming in the flowerbed near the parking lot. It felt wonderful being alive; the same feeling I remember holding onto when I left the treatment center for my alcoholism, excited to begin continuing my recovery on the next level. Folding my walker after Joanne opened the car door; I tossed it in and slowly positioned myself on the seat, swinging my legs into the front passenger side. As I closed the door I looked out the window onto the nature that was awakening all around me, repeating the words that had become so very important to Buck as he was leaving Huntington, "...*because all life is biased on the side of supporting itself*."

"What's that, John?"

I smiled at Joanne who glanced my way, "Nothing Honey; guess I'm just thankful to be alive. No coincidences in this life, Joanne, just miracles...everywhere and everyday, just more miracles!"

Joanne gave me her usual thoughtful smile, "I need to make a quick stop at the grocery store. I need some things for dinner tonight. We've got a couple of guests coming over..."

"Guests? I'm not sure I'm feeling up to..."

Joanne teased, "Buck and Sarah promised they'd bring *Maizie!*"

I smiled broadly. "Let's get some dog treats! I'll wait for you if you promise me another quick stop?"

"Where?"

"The Mt. Olympus Gym!"

Joanne groaned, "I haven't even gotten you home and you're already at the gym! What am I going to do with you?"

"Well, I suppose we could stop and get me a new pair of workout shoes and shorts as well!" I leaned over and gave her a kiss on the cheek.

"It's good to have you back, John!"

After running our errands, Joanne pulled up to the side door of The Mount Olympus Resort, Spa and Fitness Center – a small but well recognized Wisconsin resort, featuring golf and skiing. The spa and fitness center is reported as being one of the finest, and to make it profitable the management sells memberships to the local area residents. The fitness center became so popular with the locals the owners sought out a personal trainer. It was the perfect fit for Buck, and as he reported to me in the hospital, since returning after treatment, Buck had taken on his work with a new exuberance and drive that truly impressed the management. He had started a water aerobics program for the older crowd, and was also contracting to do work with college athletes. His own college work in kinesiology impressed a physical therapist club member, who has begun sending his patients to Buck for continued work after they've completed his course of therapy. Buck was running a busy schedule, but as he told me, he was being careful not to over-extend himself, realizing how easy it would be to allow his addictive personality to present in his work efforts.

"Do you want me to go in with you, Honey?" Joanne asked nervously.

"I think I'd like to try this on my own, just to know that I'm able to do it."

"Are you sure? You look like you're getting tired." Joanne looked concerned and a bit annoyed at my independence." "OK, I'll be waiting here."

"I won't be long." I opened the car door, turned my body and pulled myself out of the car. Reaching in I pulled out my walker and as I steadied myself against the car I unfolded it, grabbing its rubber grips. Always a bit stiff at first, my gait became increasingly more comfortable as I guided myself behind the walker and up over the curb, and to the door. Opening it I stepped in, holding onto the door case and pulling the walker in behind me; repositioning myself once inside the gym. Refocusing my eyes to the dimly lit entrance hall, I followed to the check-in desk where a young lady greeted me.

"Can I help you?" She looked at my walker.

"No," I winked, "I can manage this thing just fine!"

She blushed, and we both laughed. "No, I can see you're doing a great job with that contraption. My name is Terry."

"Is Buck Jaeger here today?"

"Buck? She looked at me questioningly. "You must be John!" She smiled broadly, pushing back from the desk and standing to shake my hand.

"How'd you know that?"

"You're all he talks about, as if you were some Brett Farve from The Packers. He said you'd be turning up here soon. That's an amazing story – the accident, the coma and double hip replacement...and..."

"Whoa, I'm no Brett Farve."

"I do rattle on, don't I? John, there are a lot of people who are looking forward to meeting you."

"Well, I'm just on my way home from the hospital and am a little weak. I just wanted to say hi to Buck."

"I'll get him for you."

"No, I don't want to take him away from what he's doing, and I'd like to surprise him. Where do you think I can find him?"

Terry checked the monitors in front of her. He's in the workout room." She pointed down the hall, "Straight ahead of you and down the stairs."

I thanked her and headed down the hall, finding the stairs, folding my walker and using it as a cane in one hand, my other grabbing onto the rail as I headed down.

The room was lined with mirrors, nicely designed and sturdy workout machines, and rows of free weights. Buck was sitting on a workout bench, dressed in a simple shorts and a muscle shirt sporting the gym logo, doing single bicep curls, one arm at a time as he rested his elbows on his quads. I crossed the carpeted floor as quietly as I could.

Buck caught my reflection in the mirror. He dropped the weight on the floor with a loud thud, jumped to his feet and turned toward me. "John. I don't believe it! He choked on his words, "I don't believe you're *finally* here!"

"I don't believe I am either," I found myself whispering. Buck came to me, opened his arms and hugged me. Letting go of the walker I returned the hug.

Buck immediately was alarmed, "Hey Buddy, be careful you don't fall."

"What are you talking about? I've got all the support I need!"

"So do I John, so do I."

IX

...and to Practice these Principles in all our Affairs

'Surrender to My Higher Power' needs to be my daily focus as days in recovery from alcoholism progress into years. No matter how many recovery anniversaries I celebrate, I need to remember I have no more control over alcohol than I did on the day I hit my proverbial *bottom* and had my last drink. Through treatment I came to believe in A Power greater than myself, through which I am able to meet each new day with the assurance I will not take that first drink. In continually working my program, The Twelfth Step is the step I have come to believe keeps me sober in the long term. Through the first struggling efforts of the men I sponsor and those spiritually bankrupt individuals I encounter in First Step Meetings, the pain of my early days in recovery returns to me – the pain and reality that I'm but one drink away from returning there. Every meeting I attend finds *The Steps* being read as part of the meeting's protocol. As we open, we always read *"How it Works,"* the beginning of Chapter 5 in The Big Book. Often I have to pause and ponder the full message The Twelfth Step affords:

> *Having had a spiritual awakening as the result of these steps, we tried to carry this message to alcoholics, and to practice these principles in all our affairs.*

"In all our affairs," I thought to myself, as I placed my walker in the back seat of the new car we had purchased the week before, replacing the demolished Blazer. I was beginning to appreciate the parallels between working my 12

Step Program and my physical rehabilitation. It was certainly helping me through the frustrations, like Dr. Schultz not allowing me to return to work for another 2 months. He had gotten to know me very well, and had said laughing, 'I'm interested in your well being, John – not in your having a dislocation and screwing up my reputation!' It had been a week since my returning home and I was off to the gym for the first time. My gait was becoming more and more comfortable and at home I only used the walker when necessary, usually guiding my way holding onto walls and furniture. Today opened into a crisp and fresh spring morning, following a night of dramatic thunder storms. I was meeting Buck for my first training session. He called me daily, but it had been a couple of days since he had stopped over to the house and since we attended the last meeting at the retreat center.

Guessing I'd be early, Buck met me at the door, holding it open as I approached with my walker; happy with the evenness of my gait. He grabbed my gym bag.

"You're walking mighty fast with that thing. I'm guessing you might be giving it up for a cane soon." We hugged our recovery greeting and I managed my way down the hall, Buck at my side, sporting a blue and white-striped warm-up suit. We headed to the men's private spa area, lounge and locker room. Grabbing towels for me, we slowly made our way through the lounge, neatly decorated in an Ancient Roman theme, and Buck opened a locker he had reserved for me, giving me the combination. "I'll let you get changed. Do you think you'll need anything?"

"Looks like I've got everything taken care of. I'll meet you down in the fitness room. OK?"

"Meet me in my office, just as you head down the stairs. I want to go over some things with you. Say, in about 10 minutes?"

"You bet." Buck left the changing area, affording me privacy. I opened the locker to find the often quoted AA slogan taped to the inside of the door – *Progress not Perfection*. I smiled; Buck wasn't missing one of his own opportunities. Sitting on the bench I slowly started to change from my street clothes into my shorts and T shirt, socks and new Nike shoes. 'I'm going to like this,' I thought to myself. 'Just what the doctor ordered!' I made my way into Buck's office and sat across from him at a side table, finding him having changed into his shorts. I paused, noticing his remarkable level of fitness and again said, "Recovery sure is looking good on you, Buddy."

"Thanks, John. I'm feeling great. But this isn't about me this morning. It's about you." Buck sounded so professional.

"This is going to hurt, isn't it?"

Buck laughed. "Not if you listen to me and don't do more than I'm suggesting! You've taught me how our addictive minds work. Now it's my turn to teach you how your body works."

Buck laid out a charted and well-planned program in log book form, listing exercises and stretches he thought would be effective for me, focusing on each of the main muscle groups. He showed me how to chart my progress, with increasingly greater levels of resistance both on the machines and free weights. "I'm being careful with your leg exercises, and those that might put undo pressure on you hips, but *I am* focusing on your hips with adduction and abduction workouts. We have machines that work only those muscles. Dr. Schultz and your physical therapist told me not to worry too much about how much you're able or not able to do. Your body will tell us that. There are just a couple of things we need to avoid; crossing your legs, and when you're in a sitting position bending forward to always keep at least a 90 degree arch between your torso and legs. I know you've heard that repeatedly – the two things that could find you with a dislocation."

I nodded. "You're *sure* this isn't going to hurt?"

Buck laughed, "Oh, you'll feel a bit sore and tired after I'm through with you today, but if you're actually *hurting* you need to tell me that, so I can readjust your program."

Again I nodded helplessly, trusting Buck's words and yet feeling like a fish out of water.

"So, let's get started. This morning we'll spend some time in both the fitness and cardio rooms. We'll start in cardio next door, before we go downstairs to the machines and free weights." Buck walked ahead of me, carrying my log book and getting the door as I guided my walker into the room lined with treadmills, elliptic steppers, and recumbent and upright stationary bikes. "Come over here, John. We're going to start with a slow warm up on the upright bike. I like this one, because it will increasingly give you a good workout, and not break the 90 degree limitation you have. We're staying away from treadmills. Dr. Schultz was specific – '*No running.*' So, any cardio exercises have to be low impact, with direct weight off your hips." Buck adjusted the bike seat for height and I climbed on. He showed me how to set the digital resistance, time and mileage, and I began pedaling. "We'll do about 10 minutes, just enough to get your blood moving more freely into your muscles and then go downstairs to work with the weights and machines. I suggest you always start your workout with a short cardio warm-up, and then following your weight training you can return here to continue your cardio, increasing your heart rate and keeping your metabolism at a peak level. This, along with some of the abs and stretching exercises will tighten that midlife gut you have."

"*What* midlife gut?" I started pedaling faster.

"OK, OK," Buck demonstrated, slapping his own abs and mid-section. "Let's call it your *challenged torso in need of training.*"

"Guess I can handle that! We'll have that taken care of in a week or two, right?"

"Hmmm," Buck shook his head slowly, smiling slyly, "Like a treatment plan at Huntington, we'll keep it *open-ended* for now."

I groaned, "I knew this was going to hurt!"

At Buck's prompting I got off the bike, charted my progress in the log, and we moved downstairs. A few people were working on the machines. Buck showed me how to get onto both the abduction and adduction machines, working my inner thighs and outer hips, showed me how to do some simple calf exercises - always having me chart my progress as we moved from machine to machine. Approaching the chest press bench, looking fiercely intimidating with the barbell waiting for us to add weights, I remembered something I should have asked Buck when first entering the gym. Sitting on the edge of the bench, Buck went to the weights rack and pulled two 25lb barbell weights off the rack, positioning them on the bar and locking then in with spring collars. "Buck, I almost forgot – guess I was preoccupied with getting started. I got a call from Huntington this morning, asking me how I was doing, and of course they're asking about you."

"I've got to stop in there soon. It's just around the corner and I want to see how Joe is doing. I hear from Jim and Emily now and again. Jim has stopped in here and has a temporary membership. He tells me Joe is getting ready to discharge; that *he's* interested in joining here. Joe's going to continue on sabbatical from UW-Madison until the fall term. They tell me I won't recognize him – that he looks great. I've really got to get over there."

"Maybe I can get you there sooner than you think!"

Buck eyed me cautiously, "What do you mean?"

"Remember how on Tuesday evenings, an alumnus from the center returns and tells his story?" "I always liked those gatherings; they gave me a certain sense of hope that there *was* a life after Huntington; that people *do* find their way after leaving Huntington's doors."

"The alumnus for tomorrow night can't make it, and Gerry asked if I knew someone who would cover for…"

"Oh no, nice try John, but I'm not ready to…"

"Sure you are!"

Buck reddened, crossing his arms on his chest. "Look," Buck paused and cautiously began again, considering what I was asking, "I don't know what I'd tell them. It's only been about three months since I…"

"…Three remarkable months of working an exemplary program!"

Buck took a seat across from me on an empty workout bench and shrugged his shoulders, "John, what would I have to give them?"

I leaned into him, "*Your* last three months. That much time seems like an eternity to most of them. For those new to Huntington, it may as well be thirty years."

Buck paused, "And what makes you think…"

"I'm your sponsor!"

With a resigned smile and nod, Buck didn't argue. "So you're going to pull rank on me! OK, you're the boss! You'll join me there?"

"I knew you'd see it my way. I'll be there – wouldn't miss it!"

Buck winked mischievously, "Now let me pull some rank! I'm the trainer! Now lie back on that bench and grab that barbell!"

"OK, OK!" I eased my back down onto the bench. Buck showed me where the ring-finger marks on the bar were located; the orienting balance points, how to grip the bar and to look straight up at the ceiling as he guided me through the first few lifts, lifting straight up and out over my chest and bringing the bar slowly down and almost touching my chest before raising it again and again. "I think I can lift more weight than this," I gasped almost breathless, as Buck helped me replace the bar back onto its brackets.

"And I'm Arnold Schwarzenegger! John, I want you to lift exactly this much weight until three sets of twelve repetitions seems like kid's play, and then I want you to increase your weight by no more than 5 lbs. on both sides of the bar each week. OK?"

"But I think…"

"No '*but I thinks*', John! What did you teach me about our addictive personalities? *We want it all and we want it now* and that the word *enough* is not a word we naturally find in our vocabularies.

I returned to a sitting position. "You've got me there!"

From the corner of my eye I caught sight of a very well proportioned blonde woman coming down the stairs into the workout room, looking around as if this were her first time at the gym. Long and gently curled hair bouncing off her shoulders, she sported a tight fitting black workout suit, highlighted with a diagonal hot pink strip across her torso. She caught my eye as someone I remembered from the not too distant past.

Buck was quicker to catch her eye, turning to me both questioningly and at the same time certain of himself as he returned his gaze to the young lady. "Angel? Is that you?"

She approached us cautiously, and momentarily I thought she was going to turn and leave, but instead she drew closer. She looked nervously at me and then at Buck, "You're *Mr. Trivial Pursuit,* the guy who didn't know if Armstrong stepped onto the moon with his right or left foot."

Buck smiled broadly, putting Angel at ease. "Truthfully I don't know if I'd know the correct answer now. It doesn't really matter, does it? It's just trivia."

"You're Buck, aren't you?

"Yup, and you'll remember John?"

Angel blushed, remembering our last words together as she bolted out of Huntington last Thanksgiving morning. "Hello Angel. How've you been? It must be 4 months since we've seen you?"

"Well, I…I'm hoping to have a better Thanksgiving this year! Angel tried to smile, almost apologetically."

"You look well."

Angel positioned herself seductively, chest out, her left hand on her hip, gathering her hair off her shoulders with her right. "The first three months after leaving Huntington were pretty bad, but I've been trying to get my act together with AA Meetings, trying to attend one each day. I'm open for suggestions about good meetings in the area. Tomorrow I celebrate my first month of sobriety."

Buck and I congratulated her, almost stumbling over our words. "That's great news, Angel," I said. Buck and I make the Wednesday meeting at the local retreat center. It would be great seeing you there. There's a lot of sobriety among its members. It meets at 7 PM."

"I've heard that's a good one. Maybe you'll see me there. How are things at Huntington? I imagine Maxine left a long time ago and is doing well? She's too strong-willed to drink again, regardless of what you say about *surrender*. I still have a hard time with that concept."

It was obvious she was avoiding asking about Jim, and I wasn't certain how I'd respond if she had. "Maxine?" Buck and I looked at each other, a bit uncertain how to break the news.

Angel didn't understand our lack of response. "So she's back out there drinking again? I'm sorry to…"

"No, it's not that, Angel." Buck and I again exchanged glances as I collected my thoughts. "Shortly after you left Huntington, Max was diagnosed with lung cancer. She had oxygen in the house and was taken to the general hospital on Christmas Eve because her breathing had become labored. She died early Christmas morning."

"Oh no, I can't believe such a determined and driven lady could be taken so quickly, almost without a fight."

"Oh, she was a fighter to the end! But her old heart wasn't as strong as her will. She died sober, and if there's anything she was proud of in the end, I'm certain it was that. Her last words to Jim were…" I caught myself after I had mentioned Jim's name, wishing I hadn't.

"Jim? How *is* Jim?" Angel embarrassed herself with her impulsiveness, forgetting our discussion about Maxine.

"He's recently discharged from Huntington and is doing very well. He's embraced his recovery with a passion. He looks great and already is respected as an excellent speaker in the recovering community and at the meetings he attends."

Angel, thinking better, returned to our words about Maxine. "Maxine was like a mother to Jim. It must have been very difficult."

"Maxine was deeply missed in the house, and especially by Jim, but her death provided a remarkable springboard for Jim to begin listening to and relating from his feelings."

Angel turned toward Buck, "What about Peter? He sure had some wild stories about his drinking and dealings at the funeral home."

Buck grew somber and looked at me. "I'm going to let you field that one, John."

"We encouraged Peter to look into some other profession. For a time he *was* determined to leave the funeral business. His wife was balking about the changes that were necessary, and rather than standing his ground he caved in to her demands. When we told him he needed to stick to his guns, he bolted and left treatment."

"Do you hear from him and how he's doing?"

"He's dead, Angel? He went back to drinking and couldn't face himself any longer. He shot himself."

"What? You can't be serious!" Angel sat down on the nearest workout bench. She was astonished that such a thing was possible. "Tell me it's not true! He couldn't have *killed* himself."

"It's about taking back control. He must have thought he could handle drinking again. He probably deluded himself into thinking he could limit his drinking, and suddenly found himself just as *out of control* as he was before he came into Huntington. He *couldn't* stop, and in the same sense he couldn't face admitting his complete uncontrollability to alcohol - to ask for help and begin again. He knew he didn't want to continue drinking, but his ego got in the way and had the final say."

Buck jumped in, "It's an ugly disease, Angel. It's goal is to strip us of any and all integrity and in the end to have the last word. I'm glad to see you're working your program."

Angel continued, astonished. "I've known people who drank themselves to death, but to actually take one's life? Buck, could you ever imagine finding yourself…"

"I guess it's about suddenly finding yourself between a rock and hard place. You can't control your drinking and you can't handle being controlled by it."

"So you *kill* yourself to resolve the irresolvable?"

"No Angel," I jumped in. "You ask for help!"

"A lot of good that did me," Angel glared at me and then looked away.

"You didn't ask for help, Angel. You left Huntington. I had hoped you'd come into the office and talk about the situation last Thanksgiving morning."

"I read the handbook. I went into Jim's room. When you found us I knew I was history."

"It's probably true that both of you couldn't remain at Huntington but we would have helped you find some other recovery center, rather than you having to face the world again and not be ready."

"You would have done that?"

"Sure we'd have done that. It's about *asking for help!* It's about moving past the rigid restrictions of our own egos. It's one of the main reasons we go to our AA Meetings, to get us out of our selfish selves and see differing points of view – to look into alternatives we wouldn't have imagined possible."

"Even after I was caught…"

"Yes, *even* after you were caught in Jim's room. Addiction is addiction is addiction! I've always believed that the foundation of our addictive personality is an obsessive and compulsive nature. If we begin to get a handle on our drinking that nature wants to present in another form, and those forms are many. It might present in acting out sexually, gambling, one of the eating disorders, or others. Our addictive personality it about who we are, and our recovery is about learning to live life differently so that our obsessive/compulsive nature doesn't get in the way; that it doesn't overwhelm us with its insatiable appetite."

"I guess I never looked at it that way. I was feeling sorry for myself on Thanksgiving after leaving Huntington and was drinking before the day was over. The next three months were ugly, and although there were times I took chances nobody should be taking, the thought of suicide never crossed my mind. I tried to control my drinking but began planning my drinking for the day as soon as I woke up. I repeatedly missed work at the simple job I'd found and when I got fired I began getting up later and later. I'd tell myself if I got up later I'd be drinking less. I found myself getting more depressed and *wanting* to get up later, thinking I was controlling my drinking and allowing myself to fall into an ugly depression. I felt like I had crawled into a hole and had pulled that hole in over the top of me."

"How'd you get a handle on it?" Buck sounded concerned, taking a seat on the bench opposite Angel.

"A guy I'd been seeing had a key to my apartment. When I didn't answer the phone or door, he let himself in and found me passed out next to the bed. He called an ambulance and I was taken to the general hospital in town where I was stabilized and where I detoxed for three days. That was a month ago. It scared the hell out of me. I've tried to work my program with meetings, making one every day."

"Was detox enough for you? Do you think you need treatment?"

"I couldn't bring myself to call Huntington. So far so good; it's been getting better. I have a sponsor who tries to keep a tight reign on me, and I try to follow her lead. She's working The Steps with me."

Buck smiled, "A tight reign *on you?*"

"Hey, that's not fair!"

Buck nodded, "You're right Angel, that wasn't fair. I'm sorry for that remark."

"That's better," Angel winked and cooed, eyeing Buck from head to toe. "So how are you and…and…what's your wife's name?"

"It's Sarah, and we're doing very well since I left treatment. It's like honeymooning all over again. I never thought it could be this good between us. Sarah became very involved in my treatment."

Angel looked dejected. "It seems you've got the perfect everything, Buck. You're a lucky man."

"I just try doing the next right thing. There were many times after I first got into treatment I thought it was never going to work out between Sarah and me; wasn't even sure I wanted it to. But Sarah took ownership of her part in my addictive behaviors and well, we worked through our largest roadblocks as we continue to work on the day-to-day. Sarah is going to Al-Anon with John's wife, Joanne, and we're willing to remain open to each others' needs and feelings." Buck motioned to me, "And with John as my sponsor…"

"John's your sponsor? How'd you manage that?"

"It just seemed to work that way after I bolted out of Huntington and John almost literally dragged me back, after I had gone back into the bottle."

"Sounds like I missed a lot of drama."

"Sometimes I'd like to forget the drama," Buck grimaced. "There were some pretty ugly scenes."

We chatted a while longer before Angel went to the cardio room to work out on an elliptic machine, and Buck continued taking me through my workout program. Buck was right, I was exhausted by the time I got home, and once relaxed I could feel the soreness in my muscles. It felt great – not the pain, but the feeling that I was continuing my rehabbing at the gym; that I had survived yet another difficulty in my life. It reminded me of my early days after leaving my own treatment at Huntington. I pushed back in my recliner, waiting for Joanne to come home, and drifted off.

I couldn't believe how nervous Buck was as he bolted up the front steps to the treatment center, holding the door for me as I made my way up the stairs with my walker. "Easy Buck, you're as jumpy as a fenced in bronco."

"I don't get it. It's almost like I'm reopening the door on something in my past; almost as if I'd rather not."

"Don't ever shut the door on this part of your life, Buck. Huntington was a refuge and safe harbor for both of us. It's good to remember those days."

"Didn't you once tell me that your time here was the most painful and at the same time the most joyous in your life?"

"I still feel that way."

"I know what you mean. Guess I'm a bit jumpy about talking to this group."

Buck had no need to worry and yet he nervously grabbed the seat of his chair as the group assembled around him in the downstairs meeting room. Joe was the only resident Buck remembered, though Buck didn't recognize him at first. Buck jumped to his feet as he approached him, forgetting his nervousness and focusing on Joe. Shaking hands wasn't enough as Buck pulled Joe into a tight hug. "I don't believe it's you! You must have gained 20 pounds, and *your color!* Look at you, man! Pink never looked so good on a guy! You look so healthy. Who would have ever guessed you were so jaundiced and almost unable to stand."

Joe excitedly reached in his pants pocket, pulling out the Huntington Token. "I discharged this afternoon!"

"What? What are you still doing here?"

"I wanted to hear *your story* tonight, Buck!"

"So do I," the familiar words came from the entrance to the group room. Jim walked toward them, repeating "So do I, Buck!"

Buck grinned from ear to ear, shaking his head in disbelief. The house was full. Every chair in the group circle was occupied. Residents in various stages of their recovery lined the circle, some anticipating Buck's talk and some new residents who weren't certain they wanted to be there. Buck, Joe and Jim took chairs next to each other as I found a chair across from them. Buck made certain he made contact with everyone's eyes before he began, and took a deep breath as the room fell silent. "Hello everyone, my name is Buck and I'm an alcoholic."

"Hi Buck," came the chorus response from the group members.

His first words were shaky, Buck looking at note cards he pulled from his jacket pocket, and then with confidence put the note cards back into his pocket. "I left Huntington when winter was still in full force. I believed it then, and I continue to hold onto the fact that these hallowed walls and halls of Huntington helped me save my life, and if you'll allow the process to work for you, you'll find yourself saying exactly the same words one day soon."

Buck spoke for over an hour, talking nonstop. He spoke of his and my relationship to the point of embarrassing me with his gratitude. He talked indirectly about how Jim inspired him with his courageous exploration of his feelings and true self. And he closed by turning to Joe, nodding, "And if anybody here needs a clear physical picture of what redemption through treatment looks like, ask Joe to show you the photo they took of him when he first entered and could hardly stand up. I'm sure you've all heard Joe's story, but for me it's a spiritual story – it's about being dead and being born again. It's about victory over this disease. But is it a complete victory? Joe will be the first to tell you how he has to work his program *one day at a time*; how he had to initially work his program only one hour at a time when first coming into Huntington, uncertain he could handle the next hour." With those words Buck again canvassed the group, "Does anybody have a question or concern I might be able to help you with?"

A young athletic looking man across from Buck, drumming his foot against the floor and sitting next to me jumped to his feet, turning toward the door. "This is bullshit; fucking bullshit."

Buck held his ground, "Why not stay a bit longer and we'll talk about it. Some people believe, as do I, that this is the finest treatment center in the Midwest. Why not take your chair and we'll talk?"

The young man paused a moment, turned back to his chair and fell into it, its back thudding against the wall.

"Almost knocked that chip off your shoulder, didn't you! What's your name, Buddy?"

"Dominic," he snarled under his breath.

"How about if you and I spend a few minutes together alone, when everyone else has had an opportunity to respond?"

Dominic didn't resist, but defiantly crossed his arms over his broad chest and stared onto the floor in front of him.

Buck answerer their questions, drawing Jim and Joe into the conversation. A few laughs were had and a few tears were shed. Buck related something I'd said, suggesting it's the only quotation I'd ever find my name attached to:

I came into Recovery to save my ass and found my soul connected to it.

The evening closed with a round of applause. Jim and Joe told Buck they'd wait for him in the office with me. As quickly as the room had filled it was empty. Dominic didn't say a word, continuing to stare at the floor. Buck pulled up a chair, just inches in front of him like a coach addressing his best athlete — after he had lost the games deciding point.

At first Buck didn't know how to begin, what to say. He feared the young man was about to bolt, now holding his chin in his hands, elbows on his knees trying to forcibly stop the drumming of his legs – his eyes welling with tears of anger and fear. Buck took a deep breath, saying a simple prayer in his mind's eye, surrendering feelings of inadequacy to That Power he had come to believe so deeply in as he slowly began. "Dominic, I know this is tough for you. I know that…"

The young man reared back on his chair, fire in his eyes, spitting his words, "What the fuck could you possibly know? You're obviously the fucking Huntington Poster Boy. What could you know about how it is? What could you know about…? Look, Mr. Buck Huntington Poster Boy, just teach me how to drink and smoke pot like any other normal guy! OK? Tell me what the secrets are."

Buck waited, continuing to lean toward Dominic, letting him rage; giving Dominic the time and space to exhaust himself.

Buck waited for nearly five minutes as he began to settle. As the tears began to flow from his big dark Italian eyes, Dominic wiped his eyes on the sleeve of his sweatshirt.

Slowly, Buck began again; ever so softly and slowly, tears welling up in his own eyes. "Dominic," Buck paused, thinking back to his first hours in the Huntington Office with John, "let me tell you a story."

Joe, Jim and I waited in the office talking with Dale who was manning the center. Finally an exhausted Buck entered the office, shutting the door behind him. He backed into the counter for support, crossing his arms in front of him. Silence filled the room. "I almost lost him."

"Buck," Dale began, "Don't feel bad. It was a long shot that Dominic was going to stay for your talk. He's been in treatment center after treatment center. He never stays longer than a couple of days."

Buck looked directly at Dale, shaking his head. "He's asked me to be his sponsor."

"What?" I blurted out. I could feel the smile crossing my face.

"I can't…"

"And why can't you?"

"I've hardly had time to dry off after my baptism in recovery, let alone become seasoned in working all of The Steps. I can't…"

"Sure you can! I'll help you!"

"You've *got* to be kidding, John"

Jim couldn't contain himself, "Hmmm, sounds like Maxine is getting her two cents into the discussion. Sounds like *a go* to me!"

Buck looked about the office, all four of us nodding our approval. He focused on Joe. "Joe, help me out here. Tell them they're all crazy!"

"You're on your own with this one!"

Wednesday evening at 7 PM found us sitting about the huge table in the upper room of The Redemptorist Retreat Center. The table was packed with newcomers and old timers. Buck was sitting across from me, next to Jim and Sally. Joe was sitting to my right.

Buck was asked to read the beginning of Chapter 5 of the Big Book, beginning slowly after the introductions were made, "Rarely have we seen a person fail who has thoroughly followed our path."

As he continued to read the door opened. A nervous Angel entered the room. Dressed in a denim jacket and jeans, she sported a hot pink T-shirt, taking the empty chair to my left, whispering "Sorry I'm late. I had trouble finding my way here."

"We're glad you came!" I watched as Angel settled in; Jim's embarrassed eyes following her every move. Their eyes finally met, causing Angel to brighten, motioning a simple hand wave his way. Jim merely smiled.

Buck completed his reading, and Steve the person taking the topic introduced himself and suggested he was going to comment on The Twelfth Step, and how it works for those who practice it - both assuring continuing recovery for the person *carrying the message* and enriching the life of the newcomer in recovery who is receiving the message. Steve was a regular at the meeting and he talked about how important, over the course of his years around the AA Tables, his sponsorship of those in early recovery is, contributing to his securing his own continuing sobriety. "The newcomer to these meetings doesn't understand how his seeking out a sponsor and his depending on that sponsor for insight and direction affords the greatest benefit to the long term sobriety of those of us who are blessed to be asked to be sponsors. Yet when they've worked The Steps they find just as quickly that it's The Twelfth Step that will provide them their continuity." Steve continued for a few minutes longer with his examples of how much the men he sponsors mean to him. He concluded his comments and passed to anyone wanting to add to the topic. A few sponsors in the group added their insights, and suddenly I found myself jumping in.

"Good evening everyone, I'm John and I'm an alcoholic." After the usual greeting response from the group I continued. "I've often thought about what a miracle step The Twelfth Step is. As we find ourselves working The Steps, we come to an increasing understanding about what a truly spiritual program our continuing recovery becomes. The Steps follow in sequence, and yet some of us find ourselves now and again working them out of sequence, seeking to make amends when the opportunity avails itself, and perhaps even before we've reached those necessary steps. The Steps remain a guide, a generous and intuitive practice in my life. And try as I might to fully understand, I am often awe struck at the new meanings that sometimes flood my awareness."

The old timers nodded their agreement, though it was difficult for the newcomer to understand what I was trying to say. Buck smiled across the table, nodding knowingly.

"The Step begins with, *'Having had a spiritual awakening as the result of these steps...'"* and I'm one to believe that such awakenings are neither planned for nor expected. They just happen. Call it Serendipity, call it Grace, call it what you'd like, they move us if we allow them their space in our lives." My eyes again focused on Buck, "That Grace flows through those men I've been so very blessed to have asked me to sponsor them. Certainly they don't understand it. I can't say I am able to comprehend it all the time, and yet I know it happens. Those men I've been honored to sponsor insure my sobriety. It's as we say, *'How it works!'"*

Across the table I caught Joe's eye, trying to comprehend what I was saying.

"Joe, let me use you as an example. You've been so very instrumental in helping so many individuals secure their sobriety."

Joe shook his head, not being able to relate to what he was hearing.

"Recovery becomes somewhat commonplace after the first year. We've made it through the anniversaries, the birthdays and holidays. We've made it through our friends continuing to drink or use, and our self-respect seems to center around our working a good program. Yet, it becomes somewhat mundane. Old thoughts of denial start creeping in...and they go something like this.... *I've been sober for a long time now, I'll bet I could handle having a glass of wine at dinner, or going out with a colleague for a drink after work.'* It's easy for our minds to go there, and forget the harsh reality of our unforgettable bottoms, where we found ourselves spiraling out of control into the pit of our addictions. Then along comes Joe, who for so many weeks stood at death's door, the color of old oak varnish smeared across a yield sign, and the reality of our disease quickly returns. The memory of the shaking, the insecurity, the lies and the lies to cover the lies, and the physical depletion and damage finding a body trying to stay warm and connected to its spirit...at the same time trying to continue in the denial that he's not having a problem

– drinking or using more and more of the drug to keep the demons of truth at bay, faces us head on. Joe, it's someone like you," and turning my focus to Buck, "or you, Buck, who keeps the reality of this deadly disease alive and well in my own recovery." Looking around the table, I smiled a grateful smile, "Thanks for listening to me ramble tonight, but especially thanks to the newcomer who secures my sobriety." I passed, and a couple of ladies, and a young man new to the program shared their thoughts with the group.

When they completed their comments a silence fell over the group, and just as Steve was prepared to close, Buck jumped in, "Good evening everyone, my name is Buck and I'm an alcoholic."

"Hello Buck," replied the chorus of voices.

"I had a remarkable experience I'd like to share with the group." Buck began slowly, collecting his thoughts; his china-blue eyes finding their way from person to person around the table. "Last night, John my sponsor talked me into returning to Huntington House, to share my story with the people presently seeking treatment there; some more willing than others. I didn't feel I had anything more to offer than my own experience when coming through treatment, and yet it quickly turned into more for me."

Buck paused, trying to sort through thoughts he didn't fully understand. "A young and angry man named Dominic allowed me time with him after the others had left. Alone with him I felt I was looking into the clearest mirror I had ever found in front of me. I was looking into my eyes. I was feeling the anxiety and denial I had at one time felt. It wasn't just a memory. It was as real as it was when I had entered Huntington, and John my sponsor, was sharing his thoughts with me, feeling my pain. I don't know how it works. I just know it does and I feel so very grateful. Dominic asked me to be his sponsor. Imagine that! A young man who was ready to run from the treatment that was being afforded him, sharing in our common bond of alcoholism and drug addiction, asking me to sponsor him? What have I learned from it, once all is said and done? I've learned that I'm blessed by a young man needing me to help him secure his recovery, and through my simple words of hope and guidance, he secures my recovery. I'm not a very religious guy, though I try to work a spiritual program. Somewhere from my youth I remember the scripture passage, *'Wherever two or more are gathered in my name, there will you find me.'* My God moves through you all at these meetings, and last night that same God was moving through the needy heart and soul of a young man suffering, asking me to be the best I can be in my own recovery so as to help him secure recovery in his life."

Silence again fell over the group and then just as suddenly Joe cleared his throat, "Hello everyone, I'm Joe and I'm an alcoholic just out of treatment for these past few hours."

"Hello Joe," and "Congratulations Joe" responses filled the room.

"Thanks everyone. I just have a request, and I'm hoping that by asking it in front of this entire group it might not be denied."

Joe received the agreeing nods he had hoped for from around the table, and as he jabbed Buck in the ribs, he asked the group, "What would everyone think if I asked Buck to be my sponsor."

Buck jerked his head, not believing what he was hearing, as the group clapped their approval. I joined in the applause, hoping Buck wasn't overextending himself. Buck's eyes caught mine, and I nodded. He knew I wouldn't be leaving him hanging out on a limb. Buck took Joe's outstretched hand and shook it. "Only if you join my gym so we can meet regularly, and secondly - only if both of us can defer to John if we get our butts in trouble."

I could only nod, again looking into the miracle of recovery unfolding in front of me, one day at a time.

X

Cunning, Baffling and Powerful

It's been suggested that there is perhaps one mistake in The Big Book, the mainstay guidebook of readings for those wishing to work a good program of recovery. Referring again to its Chapter 5, "How it Works," the first passage reads:

> ***"Rarely have we seen a person fail who has thoroughly followed our path."***

The dedicated recovering person will replace "rarely" with "never," and yet further in the reading we are humbled by the caution:

> ***"Remember that we deal with alcohol –***
> ***cunning, baffling and powerful.***
> ***Without help it is too much for us.***
> ***But there is One who has all power –***
> ***that One is God.***
> ***May you find him now."***

Regardless of how many years of sobriety I have, I need to be careful – sometimes even more careful than before. There's something in human nature that wants one to believe that normalcy reigns supreme. Nature seeks its own survival, and there are many terminally ill people who won't recognize their limited time, thereby making the most of it – until it is too late and their last thoughts are those of disbelief, anger and regret. Those of us in recovery from alcoholism call it by its true name – denial.

We learn to live with the reality of our limitations, simple as they are. We can never again drink alcohol. Amen! And yet, the denial of our limitations continues to wait backstage, hoping to again take its place in the spotlight and hold us spellbound in its performance and control of our very being. It waits silently. Its opportunity might take the form of any need to retreat from the reality of life's changing forces, and its vehicle is often found in impulsivity.

I noticed Buck's car as I pulled into the Olympus Gym. It was his morning to work with the college football players – guys trying to obtain additional advantage over what their small gym provides. I left my walker in the car and was carrying my cane these days – which I rarely used, tucking it under my arm as I headed into the gym and locker room.

Bucks got his work cut out for him this morning, I thought as I opened my locker amid half a dozen gym bags strewn near the benches. I changed quickly, noticing how easily I was able to accomplish a task that seemed to take forever during my days following surgery. Thrusting my cane under my arm I headed down to the fitness room, where the players busied Buck spotting them on the lifting benches. We waved from either end of the gym as I got onto the adduction machine, to work my inner thighs.

I set the resistance at 90 lbs. and sitting, straddled the machine. Slowly I drew my knees together feeling my inner thigh muscles tighten. I counted one, two, three…to fifteen, followed by a short rest and another set…and then a third.

Buck eyed me from across the gym, calling above the sound of iron banging against iron and guys grunting, "Careful with that weight, John. You know how you get!"

I smiled and nodded, thinking that even Buck wasn't going to hold me back from an early and complete recovery. Lifting my right leg over the resistance bar, I dismounted the machine and moved to the abductor machine that works my outer hips – providing an exercise that offered me the most benefit in regaining muscle strength following my surgery.

Sitting with my legs together I set the resistance at my usual 90 lbs. and began the set, forcing my legs apart, allowing them to return to the starting point. I felt stronger today, pulled the pin and set it for 100 lbs. Just as I set it I thought impulsively, 'I can do one even better today' resetting it for 110 lbs. I began slowly, feeling the muscles tighten around my hips. I continued the repetitions...two, three, four. I felt myself grasping the hand grips tighter and clenching my teeth forced my legs apart...five, six...

Suddenly I winced, feeling a searing pain cut into my right hip. I gasped for air, unable to think and feeling a rippling tension quiver through my thigh. I felt nauseous, and had to get out of the fitness center. I looked over toward Buck, who was facing his athletes. I pushed myself off of the machine, nearly falling to the floor. Grabbing my cane I hobbled out of the workout room, pulling myself up the stair railing and leaning desperately on my cane, not providing much relief from the intense and pulsing pain. Stumbling into the locker room I reached my locker and grabbed my wallet and keys, needing to get out...just needing to get away. I couldn't...I couldn't let Buck see how foolish I'd been.

The pain grew more intense and my right leg felt weaker as I hobbled past the front desk, ignoring Terry who was asking if she could help. I made it through the front door thinking, 'Damn, I've screwed up my hip!' My mind was a mix of anger and fear. I reached my car, slowly and painfully lowering myself into my front seat, putting the key into the ignition and starting the engine. The red gas tank light remained on in the dash display and I remembered I didn't have enough gas to make it home. Tears of frustration welled up in my eyes. I felt a gagging sensation as my stomach turned in on itself and another wave of panic overtook me. Difficult as it was I found my foot on the accelerator. The car jerked forward as I headed out of the parking lot. On the way home, my leg nearly numb, I inched into the gas station, struggling out of the car and balancing my weight on the trunk as I pumped the gas. For the moment I stood there thinking, 'I just need this pain to stop. I'd do anything to stop this god damned pain!"

Stumbling into the station I approached the attendant behind the register. "I'm on pump three," I said as I handed her the money, suddenly becoming aware of the shelves of liquor bottles behind her.

"Anything else?" She eyed me cautiously. "Do you need help, Sir?"

I blurted it out, "No I *don't need* any help, but give me a bottle of Absolut." I was sweating. The pain was increasing and I stopped thinking.

"Yes Sir."

I had time to stop her from bagging the bottle, but I wasn't thinking clearly. It was too late. I *couldn't* stop her. Damn, I didn't want to stop her. I couldn't stop myself. She bagged the bottle and I grabbed it. I pushed the door open, balancing on my cane. Suddenly the pain intensified; things went out of focus. Holding my vodka tightly I moved toward the blur I knew was my car. I stumbled and a young man's strong arms grabbed me, drawing me up, supporting me. I didn't have to see him, but I just knew. It was Buck.

Buck knew immediately what to do, sensing my pain. I pulled the bottle close to me, under my left arm trying to hide it, as if he didn't already know. Of course he knew, and yet I tried to keep myself from believing he could. He took my right arm and stooped to support me as we hobbled toward my car. He put me into the passenger side. I gave him the keys as I tried to find words to explain after he got in.

"I...I..."

"Not a word, John...not a fucking word!" I could feel the anger, the disbelief. He headed out of the station.

"I don't know..."

Buck glared at me, his voice frightened and anxious. He exploded. "Shut up, John! I mean it."

Buck drove as if he knew where he was going. I grimaced at every sudden movement the car made. My hip burned, like a pit of hot embers. Suddenly I realized I was holding a bagged bottle of vodka and again, looking at Buck, felt sick, not wanting to believe the surreal scent I found us in.

Buck began slowly, trying to restrain his anger, his dismay. "After Terry at the desk told me what shape you were in, and I found your locker door open and clothes strewn about, I called Dr. Schultz's office. They have a wheelchair waiting and he'll see you as soon as we get there." Buck was very matter-of-fact, almost as if we had never met. He reached for and grabbed the bag of vodka, passing it back over me and to the rear seat floor.

"Buck, I really don't…"

"Shut the fuck up, John!" Buck exploded again, spitting his words, his hands trembling on the wheel. Biting his lips he tried to again restrain himself, holding back words he wanted to level at me. We pulled into the clinic lot where a waiting nurse pushed a wheelchair out the front door as Dr. Schultz followed.

I caught Buck's eye looking onto the floor of the back seat and then at me. Horror filled my mind as Dr. Schultz opened my door. I just had time enough to blurt out. "Buck, you don't need…" He didn't respond.

Dr. Schultz had his nurse administer pain medication and a mild sedative injection, and then wheeled me to his examining room. I suddenly felt empty knowing Buck was nearby and alone with a bottle of vodka I had supplied, and a sponsor he could no longer believe in.

I felt the sedative course through my veins like an old friend from my early days following surgery. The pain subsided and I felt numb. I confessed my stupidity to the doctor, who calmly suggested, "We'll just see how much damage you can do to my reputation!" His hands moved expertly up and down my hips and thighs on the examining table, and then I was helped into the next room for X-rays. By now I was feeling better and after being X-rayed wheeled myself back into his examining room, where Dr. Schultz took a chair in front of me. The X-rays were already on the screen behind him, illuminating the titanium and porcelain implants.

Dr. Schultz began slowly. "You're a lucky man, John. As excited as Buck was when he called I was certain you'd had a dislocation. When I saw you pull yourself from the car and stand I knew that wasn't the case, and your X-rays don't indicate any change or movement in the prosthesis in either femur." Dr. Schultz paused, and his office grew quiet.

"I feel like such a fool, doctor. It was just my impulsive personality getting me carried away on the hip abduction machine."

"You could have really done some damage. Once you dislocate a hip, it becomes easier to dislocate it again after that. You strained a muscle that lies beneath your incision, causing your pain. It'll hurt for a few days and I'll write you a prescription for pain medication and a couple days worth of muscle relaxants."

"You really do great work. I'm sorry I almost screwed it up."

Dr. Schultz smiled, "Don't push your luck, John. You gave me a scare, but not as much of a scare as you gave your friend Buck."

"Buck!" I blurted out his name, remembering seeing him last in the car with the bottle of vodka. "Where is he?"

"Hey, take it easy! He's here somewhere. I'm guessing he's in the waiting room. You have Buck to thank for a great deal today."

I felt the irony cut like a sword, and just as quickly felt my stomach sink again as I got up on my cane, moving toward the hall leading to the waiting room.

Dr. Schultz sensed my preoccupation as I approached the waiting room door, "You sure you're OK, John?"

"I'm OK, Doc. I have both you and Buck to thank for so very much this morning."

"Buck respects you like a professor I felt so very close to in Medical School."

I pushed the door open and an expectant Buck got to his feet across the room, eyeing me cautiously. "I don't deserve the respect, Doc. Trust me on that!"

Without a word, Buck helped me into the car. He got into the driver's seat and we pulled out of the lot. As he braked for traffic I could feel the vodka bottle roll up against the back of my seat. Silence filled the moments as we passed the first few blocks.

"Buck, let's just drive for a bit."

He didn't need any prompting and headed out to the country and past the drive to Huntington. From the corner of my eye I saw Buck's shoulders drop as he relaxed his white-knuckled grip on the steering wheel. Finally he asked, "So, what happened?"

"The doc said I strained some already over-extended repaired muscles. My new hips are fine. I need to take it easy for a few days and then slowly return to my workout at..."

"You know that's not what I mean." Anger was returning to Buck's voice.

"I know." Again, moments of silence filled the space between us. I didn't know what to say. My mind went blank.

"What the fuck happened?"

Again moments passed, "I don't know."

"Buck slammed the heal of his hand against the steering wheel. "What?" Our eyes met, and his look was one of incredulous disbelief. *"What do you mean you don't know?"* You're the expert. You taught me everything I know. You gave me back my life. Don't tell me you don't know. God damn it, *make something up* if you have to.

I could feel the tears welling up in my eyes and my chest tightening. "I *don't* know, Buck. I just don't know."

Buck was beside himself with his anger. He pulled off the road into a rest stop which looked out over the village lake, stopped the car, reached behind the seat and grabbed the bottle. Pulling it from the bag he handed it to me. Embarrassed, I took it and set it between my knees, holding onto its neck and quickly checking to see that the seal had not been broken. Whereas earlier it seemed like a welcome savior it now looked like the devil incarate.

"Would you really have thrown it all away, just in that moment?"

The realization hit me like the head on collision from months before. I looked at Buck like some incredulous school kid, "I did...I *did* throw it away." I felt the panic rise. My neck muscles tightened, my chest ached as my heart pounded, seeming out of control. I looked at Buck who didn't know what to say and my tears turned into sobbing as I held my head in my hands. "I did...I threw away all my years in recovery."

Buck stopped short, perplexed. He grabbed the bottle and checked the seal. "What are you talking about? This hasn't been opened." My sudden panic was like an unexpected curve ball coming his way, and though I couldn't give him any immediate response, a look of deep compassion and concern filled his eyes. I felt a shame greater than I had felt when I had entered treatment those years ago. Then he asked, his words softer, trying to understand. "What do you mean?"

I choked on my words, "*Intent*, Buck...there's no doubt I wouldn't have opened the bottle if you hadn't been there. I...I would have started drinking...and...and as I realized what I was doing I would have spiraled down into more alcohol. This bottle wouldn't have...couldn't have been enough."

"But you didn't, John. You *didn't* have that first..."

"*Intent*, Buck. It's what matters. If you hadn't been..."

"But I *was* there."

"I know." I was beside myself with emotion, tears flowing freely. "I know."

"Please stop beating yourself up. You *didn't* drink."

"*Because you were there!*" I nearly spit the words, trying to make Buck understand.

Buck smiled, "Yes, I *was* there, John. I was there. The fact remains you didn't drink!"

I looked into his bright blue eyes and felt myself relax. "Buck, I can't...can't...*just can't* comprehend that I could find myself about to take a drink again."

Buck's smile remaining, he slapped my knee, and without missing a beat insisted, "What? You still have a hard time comprehending you're a human being?" He could have grabbed the vodka bottle and clubbed me with it. "Who the fuck do you think you are?"

Again I stammered, "But if you hadn't been..."

Buck's words were calm and comforting, *"But I was."*

Silence filled the car as I looked out onto the lake in front of us; trees budding and nature continuing its rebirth. It was just Buck, me, a sealed bottle of vodka and the silence. Moments passed. I looked at Buck, wearing his athletic trainer warm-up suit. "Angels come in many uniforms."

"You honor me, John. It's about time I'm able to return a few favors.

Looking down at the bottle again, "But I would have..."

"But you didn't!"

"But..."

Buck's voice was firm, yet he retained his bright smile, "Don't fuck with an angel, John!"

I smiled, offering Buck my hand. He immediately took it firmly. "It is what it is," I said"

"And it's not what it's not! You didn't relapse, John."

I tightened my grasp. "No coincidences in recovery, Buck - just miracles...always and again...just miracles." I grabbed the vodka bottle. "So what are we going to do with this vodka?"

Buck shot a confused look my way. "It's *your* vodka!"

I opened the car door, broke the seal on the bottle and poured its contents onto the gravel outside – its seductive smell wafed back into the car on the spring breeze. One whiff and I knew every cell in my body would again have embraced the alcohol once it began flowing through my veins. There would have been no stopping me until the bottle was gone….and until the next was in front of me. I screwed the cap onto the empty bottle, motioning to a trash bin near Buck's side of the car. He lowered the window, grabbed the bottle and tossed it expertly into the bin. It broke against the other glass refuse.

"Angels!" I suggested.

"No, that was just a lucky toss!"

I started laughing and couldn't stop. My hip hurt worse the harder I laughed, but I didn't care. Buck joined in as he started the engine and pulled out of the wayside, heading toward the gas station to retrieve his car.

"Will you join me at the meeting tonight?"

Buck chose his words carefully, "If my sponsor thinks I should."

Again silence. "Buck, I don't think I can continue to…"

Buck hit the brake and I lunged forward. He backed off and continued in traffic, "Don't fuck with an angel, John!" He tried to be light but his words grew serious. Emotion filled him, and he gripped the wheel tighter. "I mean it, Buddy! Don't mess with *my* recovery! We've both worked too hard."

Again there was the silence. If there were words to be said I didn't have them. "Did you hear me? We've both worked too hard for where we are today."

"I hear you," I stammered, "But…"

"No buts, please John…no buts! There's something more. There's a lot more. Something important happened for me today. You showed me what I needed to see, and you showed me perfectly. I held you on a pedestal above the rest of us. In my mind you were above relapse. You're such a humble guy and there's nothing inside you that could have created that pedestal. I did. If anything, now you might be even more approachable in my mind's eye – more human." Buck pulled into the gas station.

You *are* an angel, Buck!"

"Careful about those pedestals, John." He offered me his hand.

I took it asking, "About the meeting tonight?"

"I wouldn't miss it."

Buck helped me out of the car and into the drivers side.

"And...about today?"

"My sponsor taught me a great deal about acceptance over the past months." He shrugged his shoulder and smiled before closing my door. "It is what it is."

Joanna and I had a long talk before my leaving for the meeting. The day had been a lesson in recovery for her as well, and in many ways I sensed it might even strengthen our already strong bond in recovery. On my way to the meeting my hip was hurting, so I went back to relying on my walker for the evening. As I pulled into the retreat center I realized that I had agreed to provide the group a topic for the evening. Again, I felt a sense of shame come over me. I parked the car and sitting for a moment, practiced my surrender into a simple meditation to my God, reminded myself that the most important thing I had to share had to flow from my own experience. I knew what I had to do. I held tightly to my walker as I entered.

Buck was already at the large table, Jim and Emily to his left with Joe and Angel across from them. I reached into the center of the table for the meeting materials, including the protocol, taking my seat next to Buck.

"You're leading the meeting tonight?" Buck smiled.

"Just my luck, wouldn't you say?" I whispered

Buck jabbed his elbow into my ribs, "Miracles just keep happening."

"Hmmm...how about you lend me a hand here?"

"You're on your own tonight," he laughed.

Dominic walked in and took his chair next to Joe across from Buck, giving Buck a *thumbs up!*

Buck looked concerned and whispered across the table, "What are you doing here? You didn't bolt out of Huntington, did you?"

Dominic's dark eyes lit up mischievously, "Getting a little nervous? Dale from the center dropped me off. I told him you were going to be here. Can I bum a ride back?"

"Sure thing," Buck smiled proudly, and he had every right to feel proud tonight.

I opened the meeting, going through the protocol and asking Dominic to read "How It Works," asking everyone to play close attention to the part that speaks to alcohol being "cunning, baffling and powerful. Dominic nervously worked his way through the long passage, smiling proudly at his accomplishment as he finished.

Suddenly it was my turn to begin with the topic. I hesitated. Buck leaned into me, whispering just loud enough for me to hear, "What? Still having a problem comprehending you're a human being?"

I took a deep breath, looking into everyone's eyes around the table and slowly began. "Angels come in many uniforms. Mine arrived today in his trainer warm-ups from The Olympus Gym."

Buck leaned into me again, "John, you don't need to…"

"I owe my continuing sobriety to Buck's intervention this morning." If I hadn't already had everyone's attention, I sure had it now. You could have heard the proverbial pin drop. Again I took a deep breath and told my story. The Huntington Alumni were especially somber, and Dominic looked from me to Buck for his reaction, holding onto every word I said and every reassuring nod from Buck. I felt exhausted as I neared the end of my remarks and continued to want to give the group something more substantial to take with them.

"I remember a remarkable AA speaker who started his talk by suggesting how dismal the statistics regarding relapse initially seem. He said that about 90% of people who enter into recovery and find themselves around our AA tables relapse. Going on further he suggested that 70% of people entering into recovery through treatment relapse. He's not saying that a great percentage of those initially relapsing don't eventually find their way into a life in recovery. He was giving us the cold facts. This isn't a game. It's a deadly disease."

I paused, collecting my thoughts. "There are life situations that catch us off guard. There are the unexpected tragedies and deaths, the illnesses, divorces and financial situations, and then there is our impulsiveness. It was an impulsive mistake I made this morning, not stopping to consider the ramifications of my actions, even if I had reversed the great results of a very difficult surgery. I didn't want to face it; didn't think I could. I didn't stop to think, didn't *work* a program that was as close to me as my own breath.

The AA speaker who impressed me so deeply, concluded his remarks with words that I've always held as my benchmark, *'Truly successful people hold a blatant disregard for statistics!'* Those words continue to give me hope for all of us." I looked around the table. "And who are the truly successful people? They're those of us who continually join other recovering people around these AA tables. They're those of us who work our steps, and…" I paused, feeling the emotion rising in my chest. My words became shaky, almost a whisper. I reached my right hand over to Buck, grabbing his arm. "…And when all else seems to be failing, remain open to the arms of angels. Remain open to miracles in your life."

I looked across the table. Dominic, the angry kid from Huntington, who a couple of weeks before was ready to throw it all away and leave treatment, was biting his lip. A tear rolled down his cheek. I knew…was instinctively reassured, that the Kid was going to be OK!

Many times I think back to that fate-filled day, wondering what it would have been like had I taken that first drink. How often have we heard that for the recovering person, *one drink is too many and a thousand could never be enough?* I've heard it stated even more profoundly – *how much would I have to drink to forget I once had recovery?* If alcoholism changes the playing field of our lives, so does recovery. Relapse for a recovering alcoholic is like the mythological King Arthur, about to lose his kingdom, trying to instill the future hope of Camelot rising again in the young archer boy – history doesn't forget the promise of Camelot, and a relapsed alcoholic doesn't forget what he once had. Often I ponder how truly cunning, baffling and powerful alcohol is. At the same time I find reassurance in how much more powerful a well-practiced program of recovery remains. My spiritual reflection of a Higher Power doesn't flow from just one source. It flows from many Faiths, the mirroring of the visual and performing arts, and especially literature and the revelations of the insightful poets.

A quotation from Christian Scripture that I hold close whenever we meet around the recovery tables is:

"Wherever two or more are gathered in my name, there I am also."

Again I looked to my side at Buck, and again across the table to Dominic and the others. I knew a force greater than any of us was guiding our paths, and I could especially feel that Presence tonight.

XI

Fallen gods

I was grateful to return to my work at Huntington in July. Through Buck's watchful eye and Dr. Schultz's expert care my physical recovery soon seemed complete, though the good doctor promised even more flexibility and range of motion as the year continued. Even though I was working full time, my day wouldn't be complete without a workout at Mt. Olympus. It became a regular part of my weekday, promising Joanna a reprieve on the weekends – time to spend with her.

Dominic – *the Kid,* as we all affectionately called him, had successfully completed his treatment, and since he lived in the village joined the gym at Buck's prompting. He was a handful for Buck, though Buck seemed to have the energy to deal with his impulsiveness. There was something very impressive about how they responded to each other - Buck saw a lot of himself in the Kid, and Dominic knew and trusted Buck's direction, though he might not always agree with him at first. Dominic could give it right back to Buck if he smelled the slightest hint of bullshit. They both grew in each others' shadow.

Joe remained in the village for the summer, spending days at a time in Madison preparing to return to his fall teaching assignment at the university. We struck a deal with Joe; his agreeing to come to the club on Tuesdays and joining us later for the Retreat Center Meeting in the evening. In return we would try to attend his State Capital Square Meetings whenever we could.

Jim had convinced Emily to join Mt. Olympus, and after getting to know Angel, Emily very discretely explained why her advances to Jim weren't being received. Given their *Thanksgiving History*, Angel was at first taken aback, but given her deepening understanding of recovery and her hot pink brashness, she found her own less-than-entirely delicate way to let Jim know she was OK with his orientation. They became friends and she often and openly kidded him about how capable she'd be in teaching him a *better way!* Jim took it in stride and found his opportunities to give it back when he could. Jim was as open about his relationships outside of the gym with Buck and me as he comfortably could be. He was going slow and confided he was attending a gay AA meeting in Milwaukee on a weekly basis.

Collectively we came to call ourselves *The Fallen gods of Mt. Olympus,* with a couple of fallen goddesses thrown in to keep us honest. The name stuck. Locals, including Buck's college athletes joined our ranks, not fully understanding the original meaning of being *a fallen god.* I was surprised how comfortably open we were with the others about our dependency issues; about the challenges of our recoveries. I was equally surprised at how many questions people had for us, either for themselves or others close to them and I often silently questioned if that *friend* they were talking about wasn't the person doing the questioning. Buck's manager suggested that gym membership was increasing, and his suspicion was it was due to *the fallen gods.*

Then came the day in October I will long remember. It had been a long day at Huntington, and though I was grateful to be at Mt. Olympus, I wasn't sure how much energy I had left for a workout. I had changed into my workout T-shirt and trunks just as Buck walked into the locker room.

"You sure you should be crossing your legs like that, tying those shoes? Remember your hip precautions." Buck started changing into his workout clothes, getting ready to join me.

"I'm being careful, Buddy. What's up with you? You look pretty worn out today!"

"I'm OK, he said sullenly."

"And I'm Zeus, god of this mountain!" Buck kept his back to me. "I know you better than to believe that, Buck. What's up?"

Buck exhaled slowly, closed his locker and took a seat across from me on the bench. Elbows on his knees, cupping his face in his hands, he stared at the floor waiting for the words to come. They didn't.

I tried again, "You OK, Coach?"

Buck shrugged his shoulders, finally facing me. John, I've been meaning to talk to you, but Sarah made me promise not to say a ward. I've got to talk to somebody - well, not just somebody. I've got to talk with you.

"Buck, if it's affecting your recovery in any way, I'm hoping you can…"

"That's *exactly* what I needed to hear!" Buck's face brightened just a bit. Then another long silence; the moments passed.

I shrugged my shoulders, my voice near a whisper, "What is it Buck?"

Buck's voice now near a whisper as well, "I'm gong to be a father!"

I jumped to my feet, my voice resonating throughout the locker room, *"You're going to be a father?"*

Buck was on his feet, nervously looking about the locker room. "Hey, keep your voice down!"

"I'm sorry Buck," I dropped my voice to a whisper as I grabbed him into a hearty hug. "That's great. It's…it's wonderful news!"

Buck returned the embrace and then stepped back. "Do you think I'm ready, John?" Be honest with me."

"How else could I be with you? Hey, sit down again and we'll talk." We both sat as I leaned toward him, "Of course I think you're ready to be a father, and obviously Sarah thinks you're both ready to have a child."

"She tells me the months following my stay at Huntington have been the most wonderful of our entire marriage."

"And the problem is? You're losing me here?"

"Some days I wonder if it's fair bringing a child into this world; me an alcoholic father – even if I am a recovering one. In my child's eyes I really will be considered a fallen god. You know what the general perception is out there. You know how misunderstood this disease is. And what about the genetics? If I've passed on the genetic predisposition for an addictive personality…"

"Buck," I couldn't contain myself. "Buck, *listen to me.* You know how we joke among ourselves here at the gym about being fallen gods, but there's nothing….*absolutely nothing* of a fallen god in you. In the same sense you're not a God either, and neither is you unborn child. How often do we have to remind ourselves and each other of our humanity?"

"But what about the stigma of my child's father being an alcoholic?"

I thought for a few moments, and then stared at Buck as if I were teaching him one of life's greatest lessons. *"Listen to me, Buck!* Nobody, not anybody has the right to call you an alcoholic. You're the only one who has the right to call yourself an alcoholic…and only those you've given that right to."

"What are you talking about?" Buck truly looked perplexed.

"Remember when you first came into Huntington. Nobody on the staff called you an alcoholic. Sure we said that given the information you were giving us, you drank too much; that your life situation had become deplorable and that Sarah was ready to divorce you. We could easily say you had a drinking problem, but that's as far as we went. Somewhere along the way *you* started calling *yourself* an alcoholic. Nobody told you to call yourself that. Those normal people out there can say we had a problem, that we couldn't drink like normal guys… but we took the stand and began calling ourselves alcoholics. Do you see the distinction?

"It meant we were doing something about it?"

"Precisely…a drunk is a drunk and problem drinker is just that. The guy wearing the lampshade at the party and stumbling around, or the guy passed out in the corner have issues. There are drunk drivers and inebriates. But I have no right to call them alcoholics. That distinction is a distinction they define for themselves, and only after they've decided to do something about their problem. Defining oneself as an alcoholic raises the bar. It brings the individual into the realm of again taking charge of his life, recognizing his disease and through the help of The 12 Steps and his Higher Power – transcending it. There's a certain level of pride in calling oneself an alcoholic, because like you've said, it implies recovery. And who, in their right mind, will discredit someone who is recovering from a disease of life-threatening consequences?

"John, you sound like you're trying to sugar coat it for me. I can't…"

"Sugar coat it?" I leaned toward Buck. "Forget about yourself for a moment. Consider Dominic and Joe? Do you consider them less than whole because they're alcoholics?"

Buck's eyes looked to the floor as he considered the question; then looked up. "No, of course not – not if you put it that way. In many ways, given the struggle they faced and are still facing, I take pride in thinking they're almost more than whole – given how hard they're working their programs, and how appreciatively they approach their lives."

"Exactly!"

"But what about the general population's perception of…"

"Then we have to help change that perception."

"I'm not sure I want to get up on a soap box and…"

"You don't have to hang from a church steeple with a megaphone. Look at you; you're young and the picture of health, working with people who are trying to lead healthy and active lives. Who would guess you're an alcoholic?"

Buck shrugged his shoulders, "What's your point, John?"

"You're the perfect image of what a recovering alcoholic is – and if there is a continuing misperception among the general public, how powerful you are – just leading your life, to help change that perception! Most people want to look up the word alcoholic in the dictionary and find a photo of an unshaven guy sitting on a curb drinking out of a paper bag."

"It still sounds like you're asking me to get up on a soap box!"

"No, I'm not...but what would be the harm in judiciously using your recovery to help others? There isn't one person out there who is not, in some way, connected to someone who has a dependency issue – *not one*!
Your more than just good physical health and recovery speaks for itself. If someone suggests, they might be drinking too much, or knows someone who is...what's wrong in your suggesting, 'Let me tell you a personal story...'"

"And that might help?"

"Are you kidding, Buck? It's huge. Just your being who and what you are, and standing for recovery, will quickly dispel any myths others might have regarding their perception of what alcoholism is and isn't."

"I'm not wanting to be any poster boy for..."

"I'm not asking you to be a poster boy! I'm just asking you to stand for what you've come to believe in deeply – recovery!"

"And what does this have to do with my fears of being a father? You keep losing me."

"Word gets around; not so much that you're an admitted alcoholic, but the fact that you're an admitted and *recovering* alcoholic! That you take pride in your progress, and that you give hope to those out there who are active in their addictions and are still suffering. Your child will have a great father. Your child will be proud of you and the man you are, working to better yourself and the life of your family, in a less than perfect world."

Buck relaxed into what I was saying. "And about the genetics I could be passing on?"

"I don't know if you know this about Joe. We all know how close to death he came because of his drinking. He has a brother who is an insulin diabetic. His brother takes excellent care of himself, does a lot of cardio exercise, watches his diet and does everything his doctor suggests. When Joe was at Huntington he was also feeling sorry for himself because of his genetics. I asked him if he'd rather be a recovering alcoholic or a diabetic like his brother." Buck, what would you have said?

Buck thought long and hard. *"I'd rather be a recovering alcoholic."*

"That's exactly what Joe said, as close as he was to dying! Why Buck?"

"Because…well, because if I maintain my recovery, my chances of leading a fully normal healthy life are equal to that of everyone else, and with diabetes, no matter how perfect a program one works, one might progressively become more challenged by the disease."

"Yes! And so if you *had* to pass on a gene, which would you rather pass on?"

"My genetics for an addictive personality," Buck brightened.

"Exactly, you'll find that people's perception of you is driven by how you handle your disease and your recovery. Nothing's perfect, and neither are one's genetics. I don't care who you are. Any person who is worth their salt couldn't help but regard the recovering alcoholic as a good and decent man who has learned to live a life that all people – those not afflicted by the disease included, wouldn't benefit by."

The locker room door opened and in walked Joe. "Hey guys! What a sight! I come here to work out and find you two working nothing more than you're lower jaws!"

Buck laughed, "We're just heading down to the workout room. Get changed and join us!'

Joe smiled broadly, "Whatever my sponsor says!"

I couldn't resist taking my remarks to Buck a bit further. "Joe, we were just talking about you! Remember when you and I talked about your diabetic brother and your alcoholism; about which disease you'd rather have if you had to choose."

"Alcoholism, hands down! It's not a choice for me. I look at my brother and the struggle he continues to face regarding his health. I look where I was and where I am now regarding my health, and I have to say I'd rather be an alcoholic."

Buck smiled his reassurance, "And I'm supposed to be *your* sponsor!"

"Why, what did I say to…?"

Buck held his smile, "I'll tell you in time, Joe. I'll tell you in due time! Come on John; let's raise a few other bars today!"

I headed out of the locker room with Buck, and soon Joe met us in the fitness room. Buck was spotting me on the chest-press bench, upping my weight by 10 lbs. on the barbell. Buck grabbed the weights, sliding them in place – clanging against the 45 lb weights on either side of the bar. I laid back and took my position under the bar; Buck stood behind the bar to help me with lifting off.

"Look straight at the ceiling and focus your mind on your arms, shoulders and pectoral muscles and lift straight up. OK, on the count of three." Buck counted and on three I lifted the bar straight up and over my chest. He counted for me, as I lowered the bar across my chest and again pushed it toward the ceiling, "One, two…great form, John. Keep your eyes on the ceiling. Three, four…slow down and steady your arms. Five, six, seven…great form – one more; come on, you can do it…just one more. I pushed it to the ceiling, feeling my muscles quiver and burn. At full extension, Buck grabbed the bar and together we positioned it back on the bar rests. "Nice job, John! *Very* nice! You're form is good, your body is straight. Can you feel the burn in your pecs?"

I grunted, hoisting myself to a sitting position.

"Hey where are you going? We've got two more sets!"

"Ugh…OK, OK." I grunted as I lay back repositioning myself under the bar.

"Are you trying to kill this guy?" It was Joe's voice.

"Saved by the professor," I returned to a sitting position.

"OK, OK, just a short rest John!"

I turned my attention to Joe, "He's just trying to teach this old dog some new tricks."

"Looks like you two work well together. Wish I could continue here, but in a couple of weeks it'll be Labor Day, and I'll be back teaching full-time at the university. Guess I'll have to find a new gym in Madison."

"Hey, a deal's a deal, Joe," Buck looked at him questioningly. "You're coming to the Tuesday night meeting and if you can work your schedule to…"

"I already have, Buck. I only have morning classes on Tuesday and Thursday, and will be able to be here by mid afternoon after my office hours on those days."

"Then we'll carve it in stone. We'll all meet, have a good workout and get a bite to eat before the meeting."

"That means I'll only see you once a week."

"Ah, I think it means twice a week," Buck smiled! I've reworked my caseload to be off on Friday after 10:30AM, starting early for the athletes and returning for a couple of late afternoon appointments. I'm coming to the noon meeting on Capital Square."

Joe brightened. "You really *will* do that for me?"

"John taught me to take my sponsoring seriously. Let's see how it goes. We'll be able to catch each other daily on our cell phones."

Now Joe almost looked incredulous, "You really *will?*"

It was Buck and my turn to look a bit dismayed. I jumped in, "Sure he means it, Joe. Why wouldn't he."

"I guess I'd always been the one working with students, trying to get them to understand the need for literature, how they might enrich their lives through the great novels and…"

"And you never allowed someone else to care for you when you might need it, to give you that same sort of regard you've always given others?" Buck left his spot behind the bar on the bench, came around it and sat down next to me, looking up at Joe as I continued. "I thought we taught you that you need the support of the program, to accept the help when it's offered."

"But we're talking about Buck going out of his way; taking hours out of his week, reworking his schedule to accommodate me."

Buck's head reared back, in astonishment, "It's what John does for me. It's what we do for each other."

Joe took a seat on the workout bench opposite us, "But I'm working a program trying to remain in recovery. Why should my program interfere with…?"

"Because it's *not* only your program; it's *our* program. Your sobriety is my sobriety," Buck said trying to stress his point. "When I started sponsoring Dominic, and then you asked me…I was honored, but it's turned into more than that. I *finally* came to realize what John means when he says *You do more for my recovery than I could ever do for yours.* It's what 12-Step work is all about. Although it works on different levels, depending where we are in the program, recovery is maintained through the support and encouragement of others, through our meetings, through our sponsors and those we sponsor. You'll understand it some day when someone asks you to sponsor him."

Joe hesitated, "Someone already has!"

Buck nodded his encouragement, "That's great!"

"He's a former student who began coming to the noon meetings. Buck, do you think I'm ready to be a sponsor?"

I nearly choked on Joe's words, as Buck smiled broadly, announcing assuredly, "And do you think I'm ready to be a father?"

XII

Reflections

Buck had been asked to lead the early January meeting at The Retreat Center. We were all present - Joe, Dominic, Jim, Emily and Angel among the others. Buck was dressed in a new trainer's outfit – a black and slate blue striped Nike warm-up suit. It complemented his blue eyes and he was animated and beaming. Joe, Dominic and I knew the reason.

After reading *How it Works,* he asked the group if there were any AA Anniversaries.

There was no response from the group, and understanding Buck's discomfort I offered, "Buck is celebrating his one year anniversary today!" There was a round of applause as I got to my feet, reached into my pocket and approached Buck, who rose from his chair. I handed him the brass token, congratulating him.

Originally sure of what he was going to say, he lost his composure - his lip started quivering as he embraced me. He held his embrace. I whispered, "You're OK, Buck. You'll always be OK!" I backed away and took my seat, emotion turning to tears in my eyes. The applause continued.

Buck took his seat, still not entirely in control and not caring. As he looked about the table, the applause diminished. Dominic spoke first, proud to ask the question we always ask, "How'd you do it, Buck?" That being asked the group fell silent, waiting on every word Buck might say.

Buck began slowly, his voice strong and confident. "If someone had told me when I was struggling a year ago that I could feel like I do today, that I could live life as I do now – grateful to wake each morning and take on life's challenges, I would have told them it was an impossible task, and I would have gone back to my drinking and drugs.

Fortunately I wasn't told that. I was told that the only thing I needed to accomplish was to make it through that day, and then the next. A stranger, John took me under his wing at the treatment center. I remember my words, "Just teach me how to drink like a normal guy." Buck paused looking over to me. "John, I'll never forget what you said then. You shrugged your shoulders saying, 'Buck Buddy, it'll be OK. I've been through it too."

I looked around the table; everyone was caught in Buck's brave words.

"John believed in me when I couldn't. When I thought I knew enough, I discharged from treatment against John's better judgment. I relapsed into my old ways. My sense of security and belief in myself hit rock bottom again – worse than before…" Buck paused, looking directly at me, "This man continued to believe in me, when all evidence would suggest I was a hopeless cause, physically dragging my sorry, drunken ass back into treatment, where I slowly learned to believe again." Buck looked at me. "Remember John, it was a year ago tonight that you found me incoherent in my bedroom, covered in urine and vomit. You took care of me."

I nodded. It was a painful memory.

"You continued to believe in me! And on those difficult days when Sarah and I just couldn't see the light that continued to flicker inside our marriage, John promised me it *was* there, strengthening my hope when I couldn't – giving it back to me when I could. And when I could hold that belief in myself he let me walk on my own – like a little kid stumbling on shaky legs. He didn't only teach me to walk, he taught me to fly. He taught me to be proud, to be gratefully proud of who I am, alcoholic and all."

Buck looked at Dominic and then at Joe, "And if either of you guys *ever* think that I as your sponsor might have given you something that has helped you, find John and thank him. I couldn't… *just couldn't* have had a better teacher."

Buck paused, collected his thoughts, and slowly began again, "It's been an amazing year. Sarah is finally OK with me reporting some exceptionally good news we have. We're going to have a baby..." Before he could finish his thoughts the group erupted with applause. "Me, the guy who couldn't stand on his own feet just one year ago...I'm going to be a father. The doctor tells us we're going to have a son. John helped me there too!" Laughter filled the room and Buck reddened.

I smiled, shaking my head, "No, Buck...I think you took care of that on your own! There's only so much a sponsor can do!"

"I didn't feel I was ready when Sarah told me we were going to have a baby. And then I had thoughts of being an inferior father, an alcoholic father, and possibly passing on bad genetics. My son isn't even here, and John has taught me how to teach him to be proud of me." Buck paused again, "And if my son does find himself with bad genetics, I'd be proud to have either Dominic or Joe act as his sponsor!"

Joe jumped in, "For Dominic's and my sake, let's hope it doesn't come to that! Buck, we've still got more to learn from you."

It was a great evening; Sarah waiting for Buck after the meeting, the group applauding her after the doors opened, them finding her there.

The next morning at the treatment center, while Gerry held group in the downstairs meeting room, I found myself alone and looking through the great windows and out onto the snow-blanketed garden, as a white-tailed dear nibbled on the remaining green she found under the snow.

Warming myself with a fresh cup of coffee, I began thinking back over the last year, to Buck's initial treatment, his relapse, his returning to treatment and working the solid recovery program he's worked so hard to maintain – and shared with Dominic and Joe. I remembered how he took care of me after my accident, helping to teach me to walk again and bring me to a point in my own physical recovery as though I had never had a problem. He wouldn't have settled for less from me. He doesn't settle for less from himself. I bit my lip as I remembered my nearly falling off into the hell of a relapse I probably couldn't have recovered from, falling into his saving arms. I thought back to when…"

The phone rang, pulling me out of my reverie. "Hello, Huntington House. This is John speaking."

"Hi John, this is Terry over in Admissions."

"So, we're getting a new admission this morning?"

"No, not today, John. I just want to see if I can jar your memory. I want to ask you about a guy I need to contact – a guy who was a resident at Huntington over a year ago."

"OK, let's see if my brain is still working this morning."

"We've been doing a study on alcoholism and addiction, and how successful our former residents are in maintaining their sobriety. I just ask them a few questions over the phone. The study has been going fairly well, but I've misplaced one of the alumnus' phone numbers. Gerry said you might have it. Do you remember Robert Jaeger?"

I smiled to myself. "I sure do."

Could you give me his phone number? You can call me back if you need to locate it."

"No need – not necessary, I have it memorized." I gave Terry the number.

Terry thanked me, and just as she was ready to hang up asked, "Does he like to be called *Robert* or *Bob*?"

"Neither," I paused, taking a deep relaxed breath, letting it out slowly, smiling to myself.

"How's that?"

"He likes to be called *Buck!*"

www.ingramcontent.com/pod-product-compliance
Lightning Source LLC
Chambersburg PA
CBHW030449250626
47154CB00003BA/1189